Maxim swore softly, his searing gaze rising up to Cara's hair then concentrating on her mouth. "I want you," he said. "Even though I should not. It is madness."

The raw honesty in the confession spoke to something deep inside her.

"I know..." she said, because she understood exactly how mad it was.

She shouldn't want him and he shouldn't want her. But all she could really feel was the need pounding in her blood, fueled by the heady feeling of connection—their shared pain a living, breathing thing.

And all she could see was the possessive desire in his eyes.

No man had ever looked at her with the same furious hunger, the same passionate intensity. And before she could stop herself, she said the words that had been echoing in her head ever since she had first seen him climb out of his car that afternoon.

"I want you, too."

He frowned and tensed, his body poised, shocked but undecided, and for one agonizing moment she thought he was going to refuse her.

But then the confusion cleared almost as quickly as it had come, and he scooped her into his arms.

USA TODAY bestselling author **Heidi Rice** lives in London, England. She is married with two teenage sons—which gives her rather too much of an insight into the male psyche—and also works as a film journalist. She adores her job, which involves getting swept up in a world of high emotions; sensual excitement; funny, feisty women; sexy, tortured men and glamorous locations where laundry doesn't exist. Once she turns off her computer, she often does chores—usually involving laundry!

Books by Heidi Rice

Harlequin Presents

Vows They Can't Escape
Captive at Her Enemy's Command
Bound by Their Scandalous Baby
Claiming My Untouched Mistress
Claimed for the Desert Prince's Heir
My Shocking Monte Carlo Confession

Conveniently Wed!

Contracted as His Cinderella Bride

One Night With Consequences

The Virgin's Shock Baby
Carrying the Sheikh's Baby

Visit the Author Profile page
at Harlequin.com for more titles.

Heidi Rice

A FORBIDDEN NIGHT
WITH THE HOUSEKEEPER

HARLEQUIN
PRESENTS

HARLEQUIN®
PRESENTS®

Recycling programs for this product may not exist in your area.

ISBN-13: 978-1-335-89385-7

A Forbidden Night with the Housekeeper

Copyright © 2020 by Heidi Rice

This edition published by arrangement with Harlequin Books S.A.

For questions and comments about the quality of this book, please contact us at CustomerService@Harlequin.com.

Harlequin Enterprises ULC
22 Adelaide St. West, 40th Floor
Toronto, Ontario M5H 4E3, Canada
www.Harlequin.com

Printed in U.S.A.

A FORBIDDEN NIGHT
WITH THE HOUSEKEEPER

To the squad—Daisy, Susan, Fiona and Iona,
my writing support posse.

And my wonderful sister-in-law, Isabel,
for her help translating Maxim's French!

CHAPTER ONE

CARA EVANS STOOD at the graveside, listening to the priest drone on in French, and stared at the miles of vines owned by the neighbouring Durand Corporation covering the adjacent hillside like a patchwork.

She didn't understand all the words in the eulogy; her French wasn't fluent. But still she felt sad, and stunned, at the loss of her employer, Pierre de la Mare, the owner of the small vineyard on which they stood.

Not just her employer, her husband, she corrected herself.

Although it felt ridiculous to call Pierre that. He had been old enough to be her grandfather, she'd only been married to him for three days... and now she was his widow.

'Marry me, Cara. Take pity on an old man who does not wish to die alone.'

She could feel the eyes of the tiny group of Pierre's friends and associates who had arrived for the burial staring at her as she watched the sun dip towards the crest of the hill.

And could hear what they were thinking.

Gold-digger. Opportunist. Whore.

But she refused to feel guilty about accepting Pierre's proposal. Pierre had told her the vineyard would have to be sold. All she stood to gain from their brief marriage was a small legacy from his will to cover the wages he had been unable to pay her for months.

Towards the end she'd been more like a carer than a housekeeper. She'd bathed Pierre, fed him, helped him dress, wheeled him into the fields he loved each morning so he could watch the vines ripen and had endless conversations each evening about everything from Simone Signoret—his favourite French movie star—to the latest news of Maxim Durand, the billionaire vintner who owned all the land surrounding Pierre's much smaller vineyard. And who Pierre said had been trying to put him out of business for years.

She had never just been Pierre's employee. She'd been his companion and eventually his friend. Theirs had never been a sexual relationship, although she'd be damned if she'd humiliate Pierre by letting anyone know that. They'd struck a deal: if she married him he would be able to pay her the wages he owed her after his death, and she needed that money to help her settle somewhere new.

The pang of loss and anxiety tightened around her chest. She would miss Pierre but, more than that, she would miss La Maison de la Lune because the house had become her home.

She'd been living at the ramshackle old farmhouse for eleven months, scrubbing the stone floors until they gleamed, dusting the worn furniture, learning how to work the temperamental washing machine, planting a vegetable patch to save money on their food bill.

She'd never stayed anywhere this long, never felt so settled and secure, and it hurt more than it ever had before to know she would be forced to move on soon.

She sighed. She ought to be used to it by now. So why did it feel harder this time? Was it just because she was getting older? She'd turned twenty-one two weeks ago. One thing was for sure, La Maison de la Lune held a special place in heart.

She squinted into the setting sun as a large black SUV appeared on the far ridge. A cloud of dust rose in its wake as it bounced over the rutted track towards the family cemetery on the edge of the de la Mare property.

Probably another of Pierre's casual acquaintances come to judge her.

But then she noted the Durand logo on the side of the Jeep as the vehicle stopped and a man got out.

He was tall and muscular, wearing worn jeans, battered work boots and a grubby white T-shirt, his jaw covered in stubble.

She recognised him instantly, even though she'd never met him and never seen him in such casual attire—only in tuxedos and designer suits in snapped shots online and in tabloid magazines.

Maxim Durand, Pierre's billionaire neighbour. And France's most eligible playboy, according to *Paris Match*. Who else could look that ruthless and commanding—and annoyingly handsome—while dressed like a labourer? And who else would be arrogant enough to attend a funeral straight from the fields?

Anxiety skittered up her spine. What was Pierre's business rival doing coming to his funeral? There had been no love lost between the two men, or certainly not by Pierre. Her employer had talked about Durand often, with utter contempt and surprising venom. She had loved Pierre—he was charming and paternalistic towards her—but his hatred of Durand had shown a side of her employer she had never quite understood. Pierre had been fixated on the other man. Every time they had a problem at the vineyard—a small fire, a spring flood, one of the field hands leaving—Pierre had blamed Durand, as if the other man was personally responsible for everything that had gone wrong over the years. Cara had tried not to encourage it. She'd thought Pierre was paranoid—yes, the Durand Corporation had bought up all the land surrounding the de la Mare estate, but Durand had never attempted to buy out Pierre—but now she wondered. Was it possible Pierre had been right? Had Durand simply been waiting for Pierre to die before making his move?

Durand slammed the door of the Jeep and marched across the dry earth to the graveside, his movements supremely confident. He certainly didn't look as if he were in mourning. A strange liquid pull worked its way through her system.

A blush burned her neck as Durand dipped his head and she could feel his gaze, behind dark aviator sunglasses, assessing her in the retro fifties black dress she'd found at the market the previous day. The dress had been too tight, but with its wide skirt, fitted bodice and hourglass shape it had looked elegant. She never wore dresses, feeling more comfortable in what Pierre had laughingly called her 'work uniform' of shorts and T-shirts. But she'd wanted to look elegant today, for Pierre. And the dress had suited the occasion. Or so she'd thought until this moment. Durand's perusal scorched her skin, insulting her and exciting her at one and the same time—and making her feel more exposed than elegant.

But he didn't speak to her, his gaze leaving her burning face as he approached the graveside and said something to Marcel Caron, Pierre's lawyer.

The priest finally stopped talking and handed her a trowel. She bent to scoop up a shovel of earth, far too aware now of her breasts straining against the tight bodice.

She sprinkled the chalky red earth on Pierre's coffin.

'Give Simone a kiss from me, Pierre,' she whispered in English. Handing the trowel back to the priest, she said a silent goodbye to her friend.

Swallowing to hold back the emotion closing her throat, she turned from the graveside and walked past the graves of the de la Mare ancestors, heading down the hillside to La Maison de la Lune.

She'd decided not to arrange any kind of wake. Pierre had told her he didn't want any fuss.

Pierre's lawyer, Marcel, was due to come to the farmhouse after the service to give her a cheque for the money Pierre had promised her from his pension when they'd wed. She already had one of de la Mare's best wines open and breathing—the way Pierre had taught her to do—on the kitchen counter ready for Marcel's arrival.

She heard some hissed whispers in French as she headed past the other mourners, but no one approached her.

She needed to pack her rucksack and start thinking about where she was going to go next. She doubted there would be much time once the estate had been settled. And if Durand bought it he would want her off the land quickly. She wanted to be ready to go before she was pushed. And Durand's presence here today—in his work clothes—suggested he wasn't going to stand on ceremony.

Should she go to Paris? To London? To Madrid maybe? She'd never been to Spain before.

But as she tried to muster some enthusiasm for her new adventure all she felt was weary. And sad. And heartsick.

Sod it. She wasn't going to pack tonight.

Tonight she wanted to remember her friend—a sad smile curved her lips— her husband. So once Marcel left she would sit out on the terrace, sip Pierre's beautiful wine and enjoy the twilight magic of the vines she had come to love. The vines that had become a rare oasis of calm and security and safety amid the chaos of her nomadic life.

She could feel the laser-like intensity of Durand's gaze behind his sunglasses as she made her way past him to the path out of the graveyard. A disturbing prickle of need ran riot over her skin and the hot, heavy weight settled low in her belly.

She struggled to rationalise the strange, unfamiliar sensations.

Durand was rich and forceful, a notorious womaniser, and exuded an animal magnetism it would be hard for any woman to ignore. And she had so little experience with men. As a foster child, she had learned to hide her light under a very big bushel. It was always better not to be noticed, then you might get to stay a bit longer. And as a teenager she'd been a tomboy, determined not to conform to the stereotype of an unwanted girl looking for love in all the wrong places. She was still a virgin, for goodness' sake. Thanks to her rootless existence since leaving foster care she'd never settled down anywhere long enough to build a meaningful relationship with a guy. Well, apart from Pierre! But Pierre—despite their last-minute marriage—had been forty years older than her and frail, not a forceful, magnetic man in his physical prime.

Given her history, it was no surprise she found Durand's attention a bit…disconcerting.

But the good news was she didn't know him and she never had to meet him—so this weird heady feeling would pass. Eventually.

Before too much longer Durand was probably going to own the two-hundred-year-old de la Mare vines that produced the best vintage in the region and the beautiful old stone farmhouse that had become the first real home she had ever known.

But tonight the vines and La Maison de la Lune were hers. And she did not need to get Durand's permission—or anyone else's permission—to enjoy them.

'How long before the estate goes on the market?' Maxim Durand asked Pierre de la Mare's lawyer in French as he watched the girl—de la Mare's housekeeper, or nursemaid, or whatever the hell she was—walk past him without making eye contact.

Her curves moved sinuously in the vintage dress, the black silk shimmering gold in the sunset, the reddening dusk turning her mass of blonde hair, pinned in a haphazard chignon, to a rich gold. His pulse beat a lusty tattoo in his crotch. Infuriatingly.

Someone had said the old man had got himself a new housekeeper a while ago. He'd expected her to be young and pretty, but not young enough to be de la Mare's granddaughter. How old was she? Early twenties at the most. Which would make her up to a decade younger than his own thirty-one years. And as much as forty years younger than de la Mare.

Did the old bastard have no shame whatsoever? Despite her apparent youth, though, he would guess the girl had supplied more than just pastoral care for the old roué. De la Mare would have charmed her into his bed the way he'd charmed so many other women. She looked like just his type too. Hot and available.

But still the pulse of desire and a grudging respect, rather than the distaste he wanted to feel, persisted as she strode into the shadow of the trees with her head held high.

What was it about the woman that had captivated him as soon as he had arrived? Perhaps it was the flush that hit her cheeks as he checked out her impressive breasts—provocatively displayed for every man here to enjoy in the revealing dress—or the flicker of surprise in her cornflower blue eyes as they met his. Or maybe it was just that he hadn't slept with a woman in close to three months and he was fatigued after getting up before dawn this morning to assess the new yield. But whatever the reason, he didn't like it.

Now de la Mare was finally dead, Maxim intended to claim what was rightfully his—not get distracted by the old man's leftovers.

'Your haste is quite unseemly, Monsieur Durand,' the lawyer murmured. 'Monsieur de la Mare only died a few days ago.'

'This is business, not personal,' he lied easily.

'I wish to be informed as soon as the estate is on the market.'

He'd waited long enough to get hold of the de la Mare Estate. He'd refused to deal with the old bastard, but had ensured that no one else would offer for the land while the man was alive. Now de la Mare was dead, the vineyard was his for the taking.

'It is not as simple as that; we must meet tonight at La Maison de la Lune,' Marcel Caron said, 'for the reading of the will. Actually, it is good you are here. It will save me sending for you, as Monsieur de la Mare requested you attend.'

'What?' Maxim's attention switched to the lawyer—the girl had already disappeared anyway—as he struggled to hide his shock. He ruthlessly quashed the foolish kernel of hope. He knew there would be nothing for him in the man's will.

'Monsieur de la Mare requested you attend two days before he died when he made his will.'

'Why did he even make a will?' Maxim said, his voice hoarse with anger. 'He had nothing but debts to pass on and no heirs to pass it to as I understand it.'

Or none he was prepared to claim.

Bitterness rose in his throat like bile.

He swallowed it down as he had so many times before. Ever since he was a small boy and his mother had tied him to his bed to stop him from running through the woods to La Maison de la Lune in a desperate bid to see the man who did not want to see him.

'You have not heard?' The lawyer looked sheepish.

'Heard what? I only returned from my business in Italy yesterday and I've been in the fields all day,' Maxim demanded as the sick dread—which had been a large part of his childhood—churned in his gut.

'Mademoiselle Evans, La Maison's housekeeper, and Monsieur de la Mare were married three days ago, and she is now his widow.'

Bitterness knifed through his gut as his mother's face seared his memory—fragile and drawn and exhausted—the way he remembered her, the last time he'd seen her, on the morning he'd left Burgundy as an outraged and humiliated fifteen-year-old.

'*Merde*,' he murmured as his anger became icily cold.

The little English whore hadn't just been screwing de la Mare, she'd managed to seduce the old bastard into doing something no other woman ever had—putting his wedding ring on her finger.

CHAPTER TWO

'MADAME DE LA MARE, THANK YOU for receiving us at this difficult time.'

Us?

Cara nodded as Pierre's debonair lawyer Marcel stood in the farmhouse's doorway an hour after the funeral. 'It's good to see you, Marcel. Is…is someone else coming?' she asked. Marcel's English was usually flawless. But then the SUV she'd seen at the cemetery drove into the farmyard. And Maxim Durand stepped out of the car.

He'd changed out of the grubby T-shirt and jeans he'd worn at the graveside into a pair of designer trousers and a white linen shirt rolled up at the sleeves. His dark hair was damp and slicked back from his face as if he'd recently showered and his jaw clean-shaven. But he still looked untamed and intimidating as he strode across the yard.

He'd also lost the sunglasses, the piercing gaze even more devastating than it had been at the cemetery when it raked over her figure. Thankfully, she'd changed out of the too-revealing dress, but she wished she had dressed in something more formal than the pair of shorts and the thin cotton camisole and shirt she was wearing. Marcel had visited the house often, especially in the last few weeks, to see Pierre and she'd stopped standing on ceremony with him months ago. But Durand wasn't a friend or even an acquaintance.

'*Bon soir*, Madame de la Mare. Marcel asked me to attend at your husband's request,' Durand said with a perfunctory nod of greeting. His perfect yet heavily accented English though, like his gaze, was ripe with thinly veiled contempt.

Cara ruthlessly quashed the shiver of distress, and the heady ripple of sensation which hadn't died as she had hoped.

She hadn't realised quite how large he was at the cemetery, his shoulders wide enough to block out the glow of twilight as he stood in the doorway. The top of her head barely reached his collarbone.

Why had Pierre requested his presence? This made no sense. The will was just a formality, a chance for Pierre to pay her the wages he owed her, wasn't it?

Had Durand already bought the estate? Was that possible? Would she have to leave tonight?

Or first thing in the morning? She'd thought she would have more time, a few days at least.

And why couldn't she control the liquid pull tugging at the deepest reaches of her body? This was worse than seeing him from several yards away at the graveyard. Up close and personal, Maxim Durand was a force of nature, who seemed to have a control of her senses she could neither rationalise or deny.

She didn't want to invite him into her home. Her sanctuary.

But as Marcel and Durand stood on the doorstep she knew she didn't have a choice. The realisation made her feel like she had so many times as a child, being told she was going to be uprooted again and moved to a new family.

Powerless.

'I… I see,' she said, although she really didn't see. 'Please come in,' she murmured, but her arm shook as she held the door open.

Durand's shoes echoed on the farmhouse's stone flooring as he walked past her, the scent of expensive sandalwood soap tinged with the distinctive salty scent of the man filling her senses.

She shifted away from him, feeling like Red Riding Hood being stalked by the wolf.

Without waiting for another invitation or any directions, Durand strode down the corridor towards the visitors' salon at the back of the house where she had laid out a light meal for her and Marcel.

The shiver of distress, and unexplained heat, was joined by a spike of anger.

Durand didn't own her home yet.

Given his height, he had to duck his head to get under the door lintel before entering the large airy room now suffused with the golden glow of full dusk. That he did it instinctively and seemed to know exactly where she would have laid out the wine and food she had prepared only rattled Cara more.

How did Durand know the house so well? Had he been here before? Pierre had certainly never mentioned that he had met his nemesis in all the conversations they'd had about his business rival.

Pierre had been obsessed with the man, but she'd always assumed that was simply because the Durand Corporation had been encroaching on the shrinking de la Mare estate for so long.

But now she wondered. Was Pierre's dislike of this man, his enmity towards him, more personal? It was just one more reason to be wary.

Durand stood in the large room, somehow managing to make it look small, with his back to the butcher's block table where she had arranged an array of cheeses, a fresh baguette and a platter of fruit. He stared out at the de la Mare vineyard, his legs wide and his arms crossed, making the seams of his shirt stretch over his shoulder blades. The rolled-up sleeves revealed the bulge of deeply tanned biceps. The sun had set half an hour ago, but there was enough light to see the gnarled roots of the ancient vines that were the de la Mare legacy.

Durand's stance looked nonchalant, dominant, as if he were already surveying his own property, but tension vibrated through him too, almost as if he were a tiger waiting to pounce.

She covered an instinctive shudder by hastily lifting the carafe of wine she'd left breathing on the sideboard.

'Pierre asked that I serve the Montramere Premier Cru tonight,' she said, taking an additional glass from the sideboard.

But as she began to pour the wine Durand's gruff voice intervened, the husky purr stroking her skin despite the brittle tone.

'Don't bother pouring me a glass. I prefer not to mix business with pleasure.'

If she'd been in any doubt the enmity between Pierre and Durand wasn't personal, she wasn't in doubt any more.

'Very well, Monsieur Durand,' she managed, pouring a glass for herself and Marcel. She lifted the wine to her lips, attempting to appear calm and unruffled by Durand's surly presence. 'To Pierre,' she added. 'And the de la Mare vines.'

Durand's features remained schooled into a blank expression. But she noticed a muscle jump in his jaw when he dipped his head in acknowledgement then murmured, *'Aux vignes, mais pas à l'homme.'*

Perhaps he thought she didn't understand him, but she got the gist of what he had said.

To the vines, but not the man.

'To Pierre,' the lawyer said, raising his glass without acknowledging Durand's inflammatory comment. Either Marcel was trying to defuse the tension or he was deaf.

After sipping the excellent vintage, the lawyer sighed with appreciation. *'Magnifique.'* He indicated the chairs at the table. 'Let us sit,' he said before taking a seat, 'and enjoy the refreshments Madame de la Mare has provided while I outline the terms of Monsieur de la Mare's will.'

'I don't wish to sit,' Durand announced, 'or eat. I wish to get this over with.'

The lawyer nodded and opened his briefcase, drawing out a laptop.

Cara sat opposite Marcel, determined to ignore Durand.

Clearly she wasn't to be afforded any respect as Pierre's widow. Or even as the host for this evening's meeting. But she could agree on one thing with Durand.

She wanted this over with now too, as quickly

as possible, so she could get this man and his disturbing effect on her out of her home. She had never felt this unsettled, this disorientated and yet oddly exhilarated in the presence of any man. And she didn't like it. Why couldn't she control her elemental response to Durand, especially given his apparent contempt for her?

Marcel took several painfully long minutes tapping on the keyboard of his laptop and retrieving documents from his briefcase while Durand continued to stand on the opposite side of the room, his presence like a shadow—crowding out all her memories of Pierre.

Cara downed a huge gulp of the fragrant Pinot Noir as she waited, not caring that she wasn't fully appreciating the delicious notes of clove and smoke and white pepper in the exceptional vintage. Right now, all she wanted to do was forget about Durand and the strange sensations he aroused. And find out if Pierre had left her enough to stay solvent over the next month while looking for a new job.

'To avoid too much legal language I shall summarise the main portion of the will,' Marcel said, passing a copy of the document across the table to her and another towards Durand, who didn't approach but left it on the table.

'Monsieur de la Mare has left the property known as La Maison de la Lune and the surrounding vineyards of the de la Mare estate to his widow. Unfortunately, as the estate has considerable debts he understood she would have to sell part or all of the property. He was happy for her to do so, but has added a clause: Madame de la Mare must not sell any part of the estate to Maxim Durand, the Durand Corporation, any of its subsidiaries or any shell companies in which Maxim Durand or the Durand Corporation has an interest or she will forfeit this inheritance.'

'*C'est pas vrai!*' Durand shouted, startling Cara, who was still struggling to get to grips with the news.

The bubble of hope expanding in her chest at the prospect of owning La Maison burst at his furious reaction.

Why had Pierre done this? As much as she loved the vineyard, if Pierre had wanted the de la Mare legacy to continue the only answer was to sell the vines to Durand. For all his sharp business practices, the man was known as an excellent vintner. And no other reputable vintner would buy the land if it meant defying Durand.

A stream of French swear words followed as Durand stalked across the room. The leash on Durand's temper was off now, if it had ever been on.

'This is nonsense,' he said, switching to English for her benefit. 'He cannot prevent me from buying the vines; I have waited long enough for them. And anyway, who the hell is she?' He glared at Cara. 'She knows nothing of viniculture.'

Cara flinched—something about Durand's fury and the anger in his eyes felt so personal.

This wasn't about the vines. How could it be? Just as she had suspected at the graveyard, when Durand had appeared so unexpectedly. And when he'd turned up this evening at Pierre's request. There was something between Durand and Pierre. Something that went way beyond the business of winemaking.

Oh, Pierre, is this why you insisted on marriage? Not to help me, but to defy Durand?

Her stomach turned over. Had Pierre used her? Surely he must have known his bequest would put her in the firing line of Durand's wrath.

'I don't… I don't understand,' she said, feeling betrayed. Pierre knew enough about her childhood and adolescence to know how much she hated conflict. 'Why would Pierre do this?'

'I cannot tell you, Madame de la Mare,' Marcel murmured, eyeing Durand with caution. 'I advised against this course, but Pierre was insistent. He did not explain to me his motives but I believe it was important to him you be allowed to remain at La Maison de la Lune. And that you take ownership of the vines.'

'She can't have the vines,' Durand announced, the cursing having stopped to be replaced by steely anger. 'The vines are mine; they belong to me, not to some English *salope* who has been here only a few months.'

Cara shot out of her chair at the derisive comment. She clenched her fists, determined to face him down, not caring that he was bigger and angrier and a lot more intimidating than she was. Just because he was rich and powerful, and owned every acre of land surrounding the de la Mare estate for as far as the eye could see, didn't mean he could insult her.

'The vines are not yours, Mr Durand,' she said with as much dignity as she could muster while her hands were shaking and her whole body was far too aware of his nearness. His strength. 'And apparently they never will be,' she said, ruthlessly quashing the ripple of guilt. And confusion.

She didn't deserve this legacy.

She had been friends with Pierre, but she had only known him for a year; she wasn't his family and they hadn't been husband and wife. Not in any real sense of the word. She could see with complete clarity now, Pierre *had* used her as a pawn in his fight with Durand. How could he have had her best interests at heart if he had always intended to set her up against a man with Durand's power and influence? By leaving her the vines and stopping her from selling to Durand he was setting her up to fail, setting up the vineyard to fail. However sick he had been, he had never been stupid.

Had Pierre hated Durand more than he had loved the vines? Perhaps.

One thing was certain, though—he had hated Durand more than he had cared for her. And that hurt, more than she wanted to admit.

'What do you know about the de la Mare vines?' Durand asked, his handsome face ripe with contempt. 'About how to nurture and care for them? Or how to get the best out of them?' His gaze raked over her figure, the heat in his eyes so contemptuous it burned. 'You know nothing,' he replied, answering his own question. 'And yet you think you can take what is mine because you opened your legs for that bastard, *comme une pute*?'

Like a whore.

'Monsieur Durand! There is no call for such language,' the lawyer said.

But Cara couldn't hear Marcel, all she could hear was the blood pounding in her ears. She didn't care what Durand thought of her, what anyone thought of her, so why did his disgust cut through her composure to the wounded girl who had been called names so many times before? And why was his forceful fury only making the sensations racing over her skin more volatile, more electric, more uncontrollable?

'I'm not a whore, I'm his wife,' she said, her voice breaking on the words. 'You certainly have no more right to the vines than I do.'

'You think not?' Durand stepped closer, close enough for her to feel the heat of his anger pumping off him, and see the tension in his jaw, the brittle fury in the vivid brown of his eyes. But there was something else in the dark depths that was even more disturbing. Something hot and vibrant that she could feel deep in her abdomen.

'I have *every* right to these vines. I nurtured them and fed them, protected them from frost and fire and blight, picking off the insects until my fingers bled,' he said, the forceful words as compelling as the passion sparking between them. A passion she did not want to acknowledge but couldn't deny. 'I worked these fields for hours, when I wasn't even old enough to see over the top of the vines,' he murmured. 'And I promised myself then, some day they would be mine.'

Durand's origins were sketchy. She'd heard the stories whispered about him in the media, that his mother had come from a poor family and no one knew who his father was. That he had started out very young working in the fields, had little formal schooling and had worked his way up from nothing, eventually earning enough to buy his first stake, then expanded and grown his business. But no one had ever suspected he came from Burgundy, and certainly not from around here, or someone surely would have mentioned it before now.

'Are you saying you worked for Pierre and he didn't pay you?' Cara asked, her voice shaking. Was he lying to her? She could imagine he would be ruthless enough to do just that, but something about the tone of his voice, as if he were admitting something he was ashamed of, suggested the opposite. 'I don't… I don't believe you.'

It couldn't be true.

Pierre had been a complex man, perhaps more complex than she had realised, but he wasn't a monster. Was he?

'*Oui*, he paid me,' Durand snarled. 'The money he insisted I owed him for being born. And I did the work willingly until I realised that all he had ever wanted from me was free labour. That he never had any intention of acknow—' He stopped short and something slashed across his features, something more than fury. Something that looked suspiciously like betrayal and hurt, as well as anger.

Cara recognised that emotion because she had endured the same feelings of confusion and inadequacy as a child, on the day her father had left her at the children's centre in Westminster and told her he couldn't look after her any more.

It was the last time she had ever seen him.

As she absorbed the echo of that shattering emotion now, tightening her ribs and making her heart thunder, she thought of the confusing statement he'd made—why would Pierre believe Durand owed him money for being born...?

Then she noticed the golden halo around the dark brown of Durand's irises for the first time.

'You were his son,' she murmured, the truth suddenly so obvious she didn't know why she hadn't figured it out as soon as Durand had stepped inside her home.

Or rather *his* home.

Had he lived and worked here as a child? And never been acknowledged by Pierre?

The wave of compassion towards this hard, indomitable man was so fierce it nearly knocked her off her feet. Because suddenly she understood exactly why the vines meant so much to him. Why he wanted them so badly. And why he hated Pierre—or wanted to hate Pierre—as much as she had once wanted to hate her own father. For abandoning her.

But as the wave of compassion flowed through her, the wave of desire surged too, that shocking feeling of connection breaking down the barriers she'd been trying and failing to construct ever since his gaze had raked over her at the graveside.

CHAPTER THREE

WHAT THE HELL did she just say?

'*Qu'est-ce qu'elle a dit, là?*'

Maxim was so shocked at the woman's whispered statement his English deserted him—and momentarily so did his fury at his father's vindictive attempt to deny him even from beyond the grave. He had said too much, far too much, but even so she couldn't possibly have figured out the truth so easily when no one else had ever suspected his link to Pierre de la Mare.

'You were…' She stumbled over the words but her blue eyes were so filled with sympathy he stiffened. 'You *are* Pierre's son. Your eyes, the shading…they're just like his.'

It wasn't a question this time, any more than it had been the first time she'd said it.

'What stupidity is this?' he said, instinctively denying it.

But his voice sounded rough with shock as the humiliation that had consumed him as a boy—

when he'd discovered what a fool he'd been to believe even for a second that a man of Pierre de la Mare's breeding and wealth would ever have claimed a bastard like him—threatened to engulf him again.

He didn't want her pity. And he had no intention of claiming the legacy; all he wanted was the vines. Vines he'd sweated and laboured over for years, believing his father loved him, or at least respected him, when all he'd ever been to Pierre de la Mare was a mistake.

'Even if you are mine, as your mother claims, do you really think I'd want a whore's brat to carry the de la Mare name? However good he is with the vines.'

The words his father had spoken to him the day he'd turned fifteen rang in his head. That was the day he'd finally got up the courage to tell Pierre de la Mare he knew they were father and son. The day he'd told his father how proud he was to carry on that legacy. The day his father had laughed in his face and told him he had no right to any legacy because Maxim would never be more than a field hand, a labourer, a bastard.

Pierre de la Mare had *never* been his father, whatever his mother said. It had taken him years to figure out the blood tie between them meant nothing to his father and it never had.

How the hell his father's ten-second wife had figured out their connection, though, was beyond him.

He forced himself to breathe, to calm down as everything inside him rebelled against the pity in her eyes and the volatile mix of emotions it caused to roil in his gut—shame, humiliation, anger.

'I can see him in you,' she said, searching his face. 'Pierre spoke of you all the time; you were like an obsession of his. I thought it was because you'd been so successful in this business so young. But I can see now it was always more personal than that.'

Maxim's stomach tightened into a knot of fury at the softly spoken words.

'In his own way, although he feared you, I think he was proud of you too,' she added.

The comment knifed into his gut. Was she serious? Was this some kind of sick joke? Did she think he gave a damn about what de la Mare thought of him or his business? He'd stopped seeking his father's approval sixteen years ago. He'd run away from the vineyard that night and left Burgundy the next day to make his own way in the world, after years living on the outskirts of his father's land, effectively begging for scraps by doing everything de la Mare asked of him in the hope he would one day acknowledge their connection.

No one here had recognised him when he'd returned. No one except de la Mare—which was precisely why he had enjoyed remaining aloof and at the same time stymied all the old man's attempts to save the vineyard from its debts. He hadn't had to get his hands dirty because the old fool had run the place into the ground on his own. And when de la Mare had come to him, begging for help and investment, thinking that Maxim still wanted his acknowledgement, Maxim had taken great pleasure in laughing in his father's face.

He had promised Pierre de la Mare at that meeting that once the old bastard was dead he would buy the vines and stamp the Durand name, his mother's name, his low-class gutter name on them—and the de la Mare legacy that his father had been so proud of, and so determined to deny him once, would be gone for ever.

The old bastard had married this woman in a last-ditch attempt to trick Maxim out of the legacy that was rightfully his. And for that alone he should despise her...

Although...

Devoid of make-up, the girl's face—fresh sun-burnished skin, high cheekbones, wide too-blue eyes and a mouth ripe for kissing—was all the more compelling. And her body, even disguised in the shorts and work shirt, looked ripe for a great deal more. No wonder his body had responded to her. She was a beautiful woman. The fact that she was his father's widow did not detract from her physical allure.

He huffed out a harsh laugh, determined to break the spell she had weaved over him so effortlessly. 'Do you actually think I care what that bastard thought of me?'

She blinked, obviously taken aback by the savage tone.

He realised too late he had made a tacit admission that the girl was right about his biological connection with de la Mare when the lawyer—whom he'd forgotten was in the room with them—murmured, 'Is this true, Monsieur Durand? Pierre de la Mare was your biological father?'

He glanced at the lawyer, who looked shocked to the core.

He could continue to deny it. He had no desire to have it become common knowledge. But, feeling the girl's eyes on him, he realised he didn't want to lie. Lying made the truth more powerful. Made it seem as if he cared about the connection when he considered it nothing more than an unfortunate accident of birth.

'My mother was one of de la Mare's mistresses,' he said, careful to keep any inflection out of his voice. 'Elise Durand Pascale. We lived here—' he glanced around the room '—until he got bored with her.' He shrugged. 'Then he allowed us to live in a small shack on the edges of the estate. But as soon as I was old enough, de la Mare insisted I work for him to pay for that privilege as my mother was too weak to work full-time.' The bile rose in his throat, but he swallowed it down, the details of that devil's bargain, a bargain he had only become aware of when he'd confronted de la Mare years later as a fifteen-year-old, still sickened him. What a fool he'd been to believe his father had wanted to train him in the art of winemaking so he could eventually take over the business, when all the old bastard had really wanted was a free field hand. 'But I have no desire to claim a connection I take no pride in,' he continued. 'If you don't keep the information private you'll be facing a lawsuit.' He turned back to de la Mare's widow, although calling her anyone's widow seemed absurd. Her young heart-shaped face was surprisingly guileless for a woman who had slept with an old man to get a hand on his property. Somehow he couldn't quite get himself to think of her as a *putain* any more, though, when the disturbing mix of pity and understanding in her expression looked genuine.

'And that includes you, Madame de la Mare,' he said, just in case she was in any doubt.

Instead of looking surprised, she simply nodded. 'Of course,' she said. 'Your connection to Pierre is private, I understand that.'

He doubted she did understand. Perhaps she thought she had a better chance of keeping the land if no one knew of his relationship to de la Mare. If so, she was mistaken. He didn't need to be de la Mare's son to take the land... And complete his revenge on the man who had sired him. And then discarded him.

'If you wish to dispute the will based on this information you would have to submit to a DNA test,' the lawyer said, obviously fearful for his job. He had to know Maxim had an impressive legal team and enough money at his disposal to keep the guy's practice tied up in litigation for years over the legality of this last-minute bequest.

'I have *every* intention of disputing this will,' he clarified. 'But I certainly don't need to prove I am de la Mare's flesh and blood to do it. All I have to do is prove the man wasn't of sound mind when he made it.' He let his gaze rake over the woman in front of him, lingering on the rise and fall of her breasts under the worn cotton camisole she wore beneath her shirt.

The visible outline of her nipples had the now familiar heat settling low in his belly. He knew he should ignore it—he didn't want de la Mare's leftovers—but then her breath caught and the heat intensified, despite his best efforts.

So she could feel it too? This pull between them that had disturbed him so much at the graveside.

'I doubt it will be hard to persuade a judge that de la Mare was enthralled by the charms of his new wife when he made this will,' he said, the husky tone hard to disguise. 'And the ludicrous stipulations contained within it.'

In truth, he doubted the girl had had anything to do with the will—de la Marc had probably planned this final slight ever since their meeting two years ago, and she had simply been a willing participant. But that didn't make his instinctive attraction, and his apparent inability to control it, any less baffling. Or annoying.

The girl's flush rose up her neck and her breathing became shallower. Her nipples were so prominent now, he felt sure they must be painful. The heat throbbed and swelled in his groin as he imagined easing down the soft cotton to relieve her pain with his lips. He inhaled, capturing the scent of wild flowers and the vague musk of her arousal.

Damn, but she was exquisite. Beautiful, fiercely desirable and apparently unable to disguise her sexual needs. The veneer of innocence—however fake—was also captivating.

While it pained him to realise it, he couldn't fault the old bastard for his taste.

'Monsieur Durand, I assure you the will is watertight. Monsieur de la Mare was entirely cognisant when he made it,' the lawyer said. 'And Madame de la Mare had no knowledge of the contents of it before today, as per my client's wishes.'

'We will see,' he replied, never taking his eyes off the girl. For that was what she looked like to him. Exactly how old was she? He'd wondered earlier, but he was wondering even more now. She had to be more than a teenager, but in the casual clothes, and out of the revealing dress, she didn't look like much more. And his father had been in his sixties.

For a moment he considered that age difference. Her gaze darted from Marcel and back to him, her nervousness only increasing his desire.

Exactly how desperate must she have been to consider spreading her legs for an old man? And how could he hold that against her, when he had done things he wasn't proud of himself as a boy, simply to survive.

He glimpsed the table, where an array of fresh local cheese and fruit and bread had been artfully arranged. And the thick fog of desire finally cleared enough for him to start thinking… If not clearly, then at least coherently.

The solution to this problem was simple. Why hadn't he thought of it sooner? Surely if she had married an old man for his property, she could be bought. All he had to do was make her an offer she could not refuse—controlling this inexplicable surge of desire would also be a good start.

'I will stay to eat after all—and try out the wine—so we can discuss the situation further,' he said.

'I am afraid I must leave,' the lawyer said. 'My wife will have dinner waiting for me.'

The girl's brows lifted, and wariness flashed across her features. She didn't like the suggestion that she be left alone with him.

Good, he had the upper hand at last. And that was all that mattered in a negotiation of this sort. He needed to be ruthless now—and stop obsessing about her rigid nipples.

Walking to the sideboard, Maxim poured himself a glass of de la Mare's wine to keep his hands busy. And concentrate his thoughts on what he wanted to achieve—namely getting his hands on de la Mare's ancient vines, not his nubile young widow.

He watched an array of emotions cross the girl's face.

Concern, panic, maybe even fear.

But was she scared of him, he wondered, or the hunger her rigid nipples and shallow breaths had acknowledged, even if she could not?

Satisfaction surged at the evidence that she

was finding it even harder than him to control her responses. Whether she was scared of him or the provocative passion that had blindsided them both, he could make her fear work in his favour. If he kept his head.

Before she could formulate a polite way to kick him out of the house he added, 'This may be my last chance to eat a meal in the house where I was born.'

He couldn't care less about having a final meal in La Maison. He barely remembered living here; all he could remember was the early mornings spent racing across the fields from the shack where he and his mother had ended up, and working with his father's field hands in the predawn mist, or after school long into the night and watching and waiting for his father to arrive, and hopefully notice him and how hard he worked. And the day he had come to claim that connection, full of pride and longing, and had been left standing at the back door to meet his father—because he was considered too low-class to enter the house.

His deliberately wistful comment had the desired effect, though, when the sympathy and misplaced sentiment for his plight he had noticed earlier crossed the girl's face again, and she nodded. 'I understand, Monsieur Durand.'

The lawyer packed up his laptop and his papers, then snapped his briefcase shut. 'If you have any questions, Madame de la Mare…' He inclined his head towards Maxim. 'Or Monsieur Durand. Feel free to contact me at my office.' He laid down a business card for each of them. 'But I do hope we can be civil about this.' He gave a hearty if strained laugh. 'I think a quiet meal together to discuss amicably how to proceed makes perfect sense. While de la Mare did not want the vines sold to the Durand Corporation, I see no reason why Madame de la Mare should not lease them to you, Maxim, if you wish to carry on producing the Montremare Premier Cru in your father's honour.'

Maxim nearly choked on the salty cube of Brie de Meaux he had popped into his mouth. He swallowed his outrage with a sip of his father's famous wine. 'That is an interesting possibility,' he managed, thinking Caron was an imbecile.

He had no desire to do anything in honour of that bastard. And he didn't want to lease the vines, he wanted to own them. Because only then could he obliterate the last of de la Mare's legacy. And complete his revenge on the man who had rejected him all those years ago.

But he had no intention of revealing that to either the girl or her lawyer. He had exposed himself enough already. He wasn't usually a man given to emotion. In fact, he was famous for his cold, clinical business practices. But right now he wasn't feeling cold or clinical. He was feeling hot and on edge. Somehow he needed to find a way to use that to his advantage in his negotiations with the girl.

As the lawyer left, Maxim watched his father's widow make a point of sitting in the chair on the opposite side of the table. She picked at the grapes.

She was nervous, as well as turned on. Good— at least he wasn't the only one unsettled by this inconvenient attraction.

'How old were you?' she asked. 'When Pierre expected you to come work for him to pay for the use of the shack you lived in?'

'Ten. Eleven. I don't recall exactly.' He shrugged, but the movement was stiff. He could see that damn sympathy clouding her eyes again and it was the last thing he wanted. 'It wasn't a hardship,' he murmured. 'I enjoyed the work. And I came to love the vines.'

She took the hint, her flush igniting again. 'I'm sorry, it must be hard for you that he made that bequest.'

'Not at all, I expected no less from him, Madame…' He paused. He disliked calling her by that old bastard's name. 'What is your *prénom*?'

'My first name?' she said, and he realised he

had lapsed into French again. Why did he find it so hard to concentrate around her?

'*Oui*, your Christian name.'

'It's Cara. Cara Evans… Or, rather, Cara de la Mare, I guess.' She didn't sound sure.

'Cara Evans is a better name,' he said, oddly pleased by her hesitation.

Bright flags of colour hit her cheeks and the heat in his groin surged—which only confused him more.

'As you were only married to the old bastard for a few days I think you do not need to take his name,' he added.

'Please don't call him that,' she said. 'I'm sorry he wasn't a good father to you. But Pierre was my friend.'

My friend. What a coy way to describe the man she had a long-term affair with.

'You do not understand,' he said, annoyed by the warmth in her voice.

Why couldn't she get it through her head that he had no need of her compassion? Whatever his father had or hadn't done to him a lifetime ago had no bearing on who he was now.

'I did not need for him to be a good father to me, or any kind of father,' he said, determined to spell it out to her.

He tore off a chunk of the fresh baguette and spread it with Brie, then bit into the snack and

let the creamy, salty taste melt on his tongue—
determined to look nonchalant if it killed him.
He had never spoken to anyone of that time in
his life when he had tried so desperately to win
Pierre de la Mare's admiration and affection, not
even to his mother.

In some ways he was still ashamed of that
boy—how weak and foolish he had been to need
validation from a man who felt nothing for him.
But Cara Evans needed to know that desperate
child was long gone.

'I survived very well on my own,' he continued. 'In fact my father's decision to deny our
connection, to reject me as a boy because I was
a bastard and my mother was from a poor family,
made me a much stronger man, prepared to fight
for everything that is mine—and I will never
allow anyone to have what is rightfully mine ever
again,' he finished.

Her eyes widened but, instead of the fear he
had hoped to instil with the veiled threat, her
gaze filled with that infuriating compassion—
even rawer and more intense now than it had
been moments before.

'Pierre rejected you as a child because you
were illegitimate?' she said, clearly having completely missed the point of the disclosure. 'How
dreadful. I'm… I'm so sorry.'

She reached across the table in an instinctive

gesture of comfort—and sympathy. The touch of her fingertips was like a naked flame, searing his skin and his pride and making the fire in his loins ignite.

He flipped his hand over and clasped her wrist, preventing her from drawing those incendiary fingertips away again, when she realised her mistake.

'Do not feel sorry for that boy,' he said, wanting to revel in the shock and wariness in her expression, but still disturbed himself by the fire that continued to spark and spit as her pulse went wild under his thumb. 'He is long gone.'

Damn it, he was a billionaire, as far removed from that impoverished, rejected child as it was possible to get. He was rich beyond his wildest dreams now and wielded all the power that boy had been denied, and he was soon to be the master of *all* he surveyed... Including de la Mare's ancient vines.

She tugged her hand free and he let her go, infuriated by the blood still pounding in his groin.

He could have any woman he wanted. Why the hell should he want this woman—a woman who had once warmed his father's bed—so much?

But, even as he asked the question, his gaze landed on her mouth. Her small white teeth dug into her bottom lip and his breathing accelerated at the thought of biting that lush lip too and then soothing the soreness with his tongue, before plunging his fingers into the silky soft hair piled on her head and...

Arrête.

He drew a deep breath into his lungs to halt the erotic visions bombarding him, and fuelling the need to transform the wary heat in her eyes into a raging fire, only to have his whole body intoxicated by the scent of her arousal.

'It would be a grave mistake to pity the man he has become, Cara,' he said, but even he wasn't sure what he was talking about any more.

CHAPTER FOUR

CARA.

The way Maxim Durand caressed her name sounded so intimate, his husky French accent roughening the R in the middle. The intensity in his eyes, though, was as terrifying as it was exciting.

Cara rubbed her wrist where the light touch of his fingers had burned the skin, desperately trying to escape the explosive sensations which had taken her body captive.

He made a point of lifting the bread and cheese back to his lips, taking a bite and swallowing, then licking his fingers. But she could see the hunger in his eyes because it compelled her too.

She dragged her gaze away from his sensual lips and stared down at the grape in her hand. 'I don't pity you,' she said.

She doubted anyone had ever pitied him, despite the horrors he had let slip about his childhood. He didn't strike her as a man who would ever inspire anyone's pity; he was far too forceful, far too commanding, far too controlled.

Except…

He hadn't been able to disguise his response to her any more than she had been able to disguise her response to him. Why did that seem so significant? Why was the thought making her feel so giddy, so light-headed?

She forced the grape she'd been fidgeting with past her dry lips, made herself swallow it, to buy herself time to think—something that was next to impossible with his dark gaze fixed on her.

Maxim Durand was Pierre's illegitimate son. And he'd once worked in the fields here. No wonder he wanted the vines. And Pierre had rejected him in the cruellest way possible when he was still a boy. And for the cruellest of reasons, because he was poor and illegitimate.

The fruity sweetness of the grape burst on her tongue.

As charming as Pierre had been to her, and however much she had come to care for him, she knew he could be ruthless when it came to his business. And after what he had done in his will it was hard to ignore the fact that his suggestion of marriage—and the legacy he had left her—had been a means of hurting his son, again, rather than of helping her.

Perhaps she should give Durand the vines?

After everything he'd suffered, did she really have a right to keep them from him?

'How much?'

She jerked her head up and found herself trapped in Durand's intense golden-brown gaze again. 'Excuse me?'

'How much do you want to disappear? I am a rich man and I can be generous. You're clearly a woman who appreciates the value of money and I respect that...' His gaze dropped to her breasts, and lingered, before rising back to her face. The contempt in his gaze was so clear—and so brutal—it shocked her.

Her back straightened, even as her nipples squeezed into tight points of need.

'I don't want your money,' she said as she wrapped her shirt around herself, attempting to hide her physical response to him.

'Really?' His sensual lips lifted into a cynical smile and she felt like Little Red again, being baited by the wolf. 'Even if I offered you half a million euros to disappear, which is considerably more than the property is worth?'

'Yes,' she said, releasing the breath held hostage in her lungs.

She didn't want his money. Only moments ago she had been considering giving him the vines. But she wanted to be able to stay at La Maison de la Lune.

She didn't want to have to disappear. Again.

How many times had she been forced to do that in the past? Because of the whims of others. Whatever his motives, Pierre had given her the house she had come to love. And she had earned this chance. 'I want to stay living here, as Pierre planned. But I'd be more than happy to lease the vines to you, as Marcel suggested.'

His smile flatlined. 'I don't wish to lease them; I wish to own them. And you can't remain here, as I intend to demolish this place.'

'But… What? Why?' She jumped from her seat, distressed not just by the suggestion but the chilling conviction in his tone. 'Why would you do that?'

He stood too, the cynicism replaced by a thunderous frown. 'I do not have to explain my reasons to you.'

She crossed her arms over her chest to try to stop the trembling in her limbs—and to disguise the ache in her treacherous nipples. 'Well, you can't demolish La Maison de la Lune because it belongs to me.'

'And once I have challenged the will, it will belong to me.'

He was actually serious. She stared, trying to gauge why he would do such a thing. Pierre had treated him appallingly, she understood that. But he'd said himself he wasn't that rejected boy any more. And what was the point of obliterating the legacy of a dead man?

'But you can't,' she pleaded again. 'La Maison is beautiful…' She let her gaze roam over the old furniture, the worn armchairs and sturdy table, the beautiful vista beyond—not just of the old vineyard, but the ancient forest that rimmed the property, the small stream that bisected the land, gilded now by the full moon. 'It deserves to be here for generations to come.'

'No, it doesn't. The only thing that matters are the vines.'

He walked around the table, bearing down on her, making her more aware of his strength, his size. But, instead of feeling intimidated, she felt energised, exhilarated, mesmerised by the fierce passion in his eyes.

Was it for the grapes? It had to be, but why then did his passion feel as if it were infecting her body, rushing like wildfire over her skin, making the hot sweet spot between her thighs burn?

'If you knew anything about viniculture, Cara, you would understand,' he said, saying her name again like a caress, the harsh cynical anger morphing into something rough and raw with a devastating promise. 'The soil here is unique, rich in complex minerals that give a specific flavour to the grapes.'

The thickness in his throat seemed to echo in

the deepest reaches of her body. She didn't know what was happening to her. But for the first time ever she felt truly seen.

He cupped her face, the rough calluses on his palm making her shudder as his thumb brushed across her lips. She should step back, away from that incendiary passion, but she felt trapped, owned and so desperately needy, the pulse between her thighs spreading out to ignite her entire body.

'Once I own the vines,' he murmured, 'I can propagate them and replant on the land, creating a new vintage, even better than the Montremere.'

She was breathing heavily, they both were. She licked her dry lips and the passion in his eyes exploded, darkening the pupils to black. She felt the answering explosion in her sex.

But, instead of drawing her closer, his hand began to slip from her cheek.

The need seemed to spring from nowhere, more than passion, more than desire. Something deep and elemental, that probably went all the way back to that rejected girl.

And in that split second all she could see was the boy he had been too. The child who had been rejected and betrayed and exploited. She covered his hand with hers, the way she had attempted to do before at the table, to comfort him.

But this time comfort wasn't the only thing she felt. She didn't want to lose his touch.

Lifting on tiptoe, she placed her lips on his, needing to strengthen that connection, wanting to feed the hunger so she could obliterate his pain. And her own.

She heard him groan, but then his hands were gripping her cheeks, pulling her against him and his mouth was on hers.

Wild, hungry, demanding.

Her mouth opened on a gasp and he captured the sob as he angled her head, giving him better access. Her own hands dropped from his face and she found herself clinging to him, her fingers fisting in his linen shirt. She shuddered, too aware of the overwhelming heat of his body, the press of his chest against her swollen breasts, her thrusting nipples becoming more engorged as she rubbed against the muscular strength like a cat desperate to be stroked.

His tongue branded the secret recesses of her mouth. She tried to respond in tentative darts and licks. She had no idea what she was doing, all she knew was she needed more of his taste, his passion, his heat. His fingers threaded into her hair, releasing the pins she'd used to keep the wild mass aloft. She could hear them scattering on the stone flooring, hear the pounding rush of the blood pumping around her over-sensitised body and plunging into her sex.

At last he yanked his mouth free. His dark eyes stared down at her, his expression stunned. But not as stunned as she felt.

He swore softly, the searing gaze rising up to her hair then concentrating on her mouth. 'I want you,' he said. 'Even though I should not. It is madness.'

The raw honesty in the confession spoke to something deep inside her.

'I know…' she said, because she understood exactly how mad it was.

They were in Pierre's house. A house Durand wanted to destroy, a house she had come to love, on the day of Pierre's funeral and she was Pierre's widow. She shouldn't want him and he shouldn't want her. But all she could really feel was the need pounding in her blood, fuelled by the heady feeling of connection—their shared pain a living, breathing thing.

And all she could see was the possessive desire in his eyes.

No man had ever looked at her with that furious hunger, that passionate intensity. And, before she could stop herself, she said the words that had been echoing in her head ever since she first saw him climb out of his Jeep that afternoon.

'I want you too.'

He frowned, and tensed, his body poised, shocked but undecided, and for one agonising moment she thought he was going to refuse her.

But then the confusion cleared, almost as quickly as it had come, and he scooped her into his arms.

'*Bien*,' he murmured.

She grasped his neck, struggling to catch her breath as he strode out of the room and down the hallway. He took the stairs two at a time to the first landing.

'Show me to a room you did not share with de la Mare,' he demanded, his voice gruff and broaching no argument.

The answer was simple. She pointed to her own bedroom at the end of the landing—the one she'd lived in ever since becoming Pierre's house-keeper.

He kicked open the door and flicked on the light with his elbow, then let her down beside the narrow double bed.

She stood trembling, her body like a leaf being buffeted by the winds of her own desire. She'd never felt this way before, excited, exhilarated, out of control.

He cupped her cheek, pressed a kiss to her lips, his large hand slipping down to cradle her neck and drag her against him. His lips devoured her cheek, her chin, the rioting pulse in her collarbone, sending the unbearable need darting into her sex, her breasts, and everywhere his mouth conquered.

He wrapped an arm around her limp body, tugging her against the hard line of his, and the thick evidence of his arousal pressed into her quivering belly through their clothes.

His hands were frantic but gentle as he tugged off her shirt, skimmed his fingers under the cotton camisole. Her bra released with a sharp snap and he drew away to watch her reaction as his thumbs found her aching nipples beneath the soft cotton. The tight peaks swelled and hardened as he played with them—circling and plucking and making them ache even more.

'I need to see you,' he groaned.

She nodded, not sure if he was asking a question or making a demand. But, before she had a chance to second-guess herself, he had stripped off her bra and camisole. And she stood naked from the waist up.

'*Trop belle,*' he murmured, the reverent growl making her feel truly beautiful for the first time in her life.

He cupped the underside of one breast in his callused palm and then bowed his dark head to capture the ripe, throbbing peak in his lips.

She sunk her fingers into his hair, the sensations so exquisite as he suckled her that a raw moan broke from her lips.

He teased and tortured her, circling the areola with his tongue, nipping at the swollen peak then drawing it deep into his mouth, the hot suction driving her wild. Her moans became sobs, her fingers fisting in the silky locks of his hair to draw him closer, demanding he give her more. The fire sparked and sizzled in her sex, threatening to consume her.

'Please… I need…' What did she need? She didn't even know.

'Tell me what is good for you,' he rasped in her ear, hugging her trembling body close, notching the ridge of his erection against the melting spot between her thighs.

The heat swelled and strengthened, but not enough…she needed to feel him, his strength, his hardness, filling the empty spaces inside her.

'I need you naked too,' she managed, shocking herself with the explicit request.

He chuckled, the sound harsh. '*Mais oui*, Cara.'

Placing a last kiss on the crest of her breast, he drew away to strip off his shirt.

His chest was as broad and strong and magnificent as the rest of him. She devoured the sight of him, so bold and unashamed in the yellow glow from the ancient light fixture.

The defined muscles of his pecs and the brown

discs of his nipples were scattered with hair that arrowed down in a thin line bisecting the ridges of his abdominal muscles. She folded her arms over her breasts, trying to hold onto her sanity as he unbuttoned his trousers. Her heart slammed into her throat and pounded harder in her sex as he kicked them off and then lowered the stretchy black boxer shorts.

The massive erection sprang free from the nest of hair at his groin.

She'd never seen a naked man in his physical prime before, and certainly not one who was fully aroused.

She swallowed heavily, unable to take her eyes off the hard shaft, which thrust up towards his belly button, so long and thick.

How on earth was that supposed to fit inside her? But, even as the panic rippled through her, her sex moistened and softened, the muscles tensing and releasing in anticipation.

She didn't know if she could take something so huge, but she wanted to try.

'Cara?' he murmured as he nudged her chin up, forcing her gaze to meet his. '*Ça va?*' he asked, the flash of concern crossing his face making her heart thud against her ribs.

She nodded. 'Can I…? Can I touch it?'

Creases appeared in the tanned skin at the corners of his eyes, the dark depths sparkling with amusement as his lips quirked in a curious half smile. 'Of course—you do not need to ask permission.'

She nodded again, cursing her inexperience. She didn't want him to know he was her first. Didn't want him to suspect what a big deal this was to her. Because it was not a big deal to him.

Reaching out, she touched his erection. Her fingertip glided along the rigid length, exploring the velvet softness of his skin, the hardness beneath.

The erection jumped against her palm, thrilling her. He let out a rough groan as her thumb glided across the broad tip, gathering the bead of moisture that seeped from the slit.

He grasped her wrist. '*Arrête*, Cara. You are killing me,' he said as he lifted her fingers to his mouth and kissed them. The sight was so erotic her breath seized in her lungs. How could she be this turned on and not dissolve into a puddle?

Releasing her hand, he dipped his head. 'Take off your shorts, *ma petite*,' he said, the gruff endearment caressing her senses. 'I cannot wait much longer to be inside you.'

She fumbled, her fingers trembling, and couldn't seem to get the buttons free.

Brushing her hands away, he knelt in front of her and released the fastenings to draw the rough denim down her legs. She stepped out of her shorts, placing her hand on his shoulder to keep her balance, so shaky now she knew she needed to get to the bed before she collapsed.

But, before she had a chance to move, he stood and lifted her easily into his arms. She knew she wasn't particularly light but she felt fragile and even precious as he placed her gently on the bed.

He loomed over her, his broad shoulders cutting out the light, his lips finding hers again, the kisses more demanding now, more insistent. The atmosphere changed. Not tender and seeking, but urgent and relentless.

He cupped her sex, his fingers exploring the slick swollen folds. She bucked against his touch, the pleasure becoming raw and jagged as two blunt fingers pressed inside her. The tight needy flesh stretched, making the throbbing ache pound so hard in her veins she thought she might pass out.

And then his thumb found the very centre of her struggle, gliding over the hot, wet nub, circling and flicking until she was riding his hand, holding onto his shoulders for purchase.

'Yes…yes!' she sobbed, unable to control the pleasure battering her body.

'Come for me, Cara,' he commanded and her body obeyed, the coil at her centre tightening to pain and then releasing in a shattered gush of sensation.

She opened her eyes to find him watching her. She was dazed, disorientated, the waves still ebbing through her as the pleasure rippled throughout her body, startling in its intensity.

She'd pleasured herself before, but it had never felt this good, this right, this devastating.

He looked dazed too, but then the shadows cleared to be replaced with a fierce, desperate need. He grasped her hips, angling her pelvis as the large head of his penis probed, demanding entry.

'Open for me,' he said. And again she obeyed instinctively, hooking her legs around his waist, opening herself fully for the onslaught, so desperate now to feel the thick length inside her she was ready to beg.

He surged deep in one hard thrust.

The pleasure turned instantly to rending pain, the heavy weight tearing her fragile tissue.

She stiffened, biting into her lip, her nails scoring his back to contain the shocked cry which would give her away.

But she knew it was already too late when he stilled. His face was rigid with shock, his gaze sharp with accusation as it locked on hers.

'*Es-tu vierge?*' he said, his English deserting him.

Are you a virgin?

She turned away from his probing gaze, wanting to lie but unable to get the words out with his erection still lodged so deep inside her she felt conquered, owned.

He grasped her chin and forced her gaze back to his.

'Tell me, how is this possible?'

Maxim couldn't focus, he could hardly talk, her body clasped so tight around him it was like a vice. A hot, sweet, unbearably pleasurable vice, about to tip him over the edge. He wanted to move, to dig deeper, to find the place that would make her moan and beg again. But he resisted the urge to thrust into the tight, wet warmth. And forced his mind to engage.

The guilty shadow in her eyes told a shocking story.

Her innocence, her inexperience, that strange feeling of something not being right that had assailed him as soon as he had brought her upstairs. The blush suffusing her ripe body, the shocked gasp as his lips closed over her nipple and suckled, the jolt of adrenaline as her fingers fumbled with her shorts. He'd assumed it was all an act, a beguiling, artless act that had captivated him even though he knew it couldn't be real. And now to find it was all true?

He shuddered, still lodged inside her.

She didn't speak, didn't answer his accusation,

her eyes glassy with shock, but there was only one explanation. The marriage had been a sham. A trick in more ways than one.

He should withdraw. But he could still feel the pulse of her pleasure, the tight clasp of her body milking him, and the relentless need hammered at the base of his spine.

'Am I hurting you?' he asked, unable to withdraw, not caring any more about her reasons, her complicity in his father's scheme.

She shook her head. 'It's... You're so big, but it doesn't hurt so much now.' She stumbled over the words. And he found himself cradling her cheek, feeling the heat of her humiliation.

Maybe that was faked too, but he didn't think so, as he drew his thumb across the full lips, felt her body relax a little.

'I need to move,' he said, deciding all that mattered now was feeding this hunger. The questions could wait because he couldn't focus on anything but the spasming grip of her muscles threatening to drive him insane if he didn't rock his hips.

She nodded. But a tear leaked from the corner of her eye. He brushed it away with his thumb.

'Why are you crying?'

'I... I've never felt this way before,' she said, the honesty in her pure blue eyes pushing at his chest. Surely this couldn't be faked, this intensity, this desperation, this emotional upheaval. Did she feel it too? And what the hell did it mean?

But even as the panic ricocheted against his ribs, he dismissed it.

This wasn't an emotional connection, this was just sex. And an insane chemistry that had exploded between them from the first moment he'd laid eyes on her.

He eased out of her then pressed back in, slowly, carefully, feeling her tight flesh soften to receive him more easily this time. She moaned, her fingers clinging to his shoulders, as if he were the only stable thing in the middle of the storm consuming them. As he withdrew and pressed into her again, her back arched, bringing her sex up to meet his invasion, welcoming it, revelling in his possession.

He began to rock his hips, in, out…slowly at first, establishing a rhythm that would satisfy them both. But as her moans became pants, her pants became sobs, the frenzy overtook him— and one shocking realisation charged through his brain.

He was the first man to touch her, to taste her, to feast on her fragrant flesh, to hear her sob in his ear as she surrendered to him.

The surge of possessiveness, the need to claim her overwhelmed him as his smooth moves became clumsy, faster and more frantic, the thrusts deeper and more demanding. His fingers dug into her hips as he clung onto his own climax, needing her to shatter first.

Her body bowed back and she cried out, the spasms of her orgasm gripping him as she flew over that final peak.

He let go at last, to tumble over that high ledge behind her, the climax shattering him, as his mind blanked and his body became boneless. And one word reverberated in his head.

Mine.

CHAPTER FIVE

AS THE BLISSFUL wave of afterglow cleared, Cara lay staring at the crack in the ceiling moulding, the crack she'd mapped each night before she fell asleep, for the last eleven months. But tonight everything was different.

The musky scent of sex and sweat surrounded her. The heavy weight of Maxim Durand's body pressed hers into the old mattress as the thick length of him pulsed inside her tender sex.

She dragged in a shattered breath and sunk her teeth into her bottom lip to control the stinging tears that threatened to spill over the lids.

But there was no controlling the emotion sitting on her chest like a stone and threatening to crush her ribs.

What had she done? And why?

How could she have slept with her husband's biggest rival on the day of his funeral? The man who was threatening to destroy La Maison de la Lune?

She shifted under Durand's weight, gently shoving his shoulder blade, which was digging into her collarbone. She needed to get away from him. He was still firm, still *huge,* inside her— and all she wanted to do right now was curl up into a tight ball and die.

He groaned and shifted and she gasped, unable to disguise the tenderness in her sex as he eased out of her, ashamed of the renewed prickle of yearning.

'*Pardon,*' he murmured as he rolled off her.

She edged across the bed, every part of her aching now, but most of all her heart.

What Pierre had done to Maxim all those years ago was wrong, terribly wrong. But surely what she had just done was even worse.

As she tried to leave the bed Maxim Durand's hand shot out and grasped hold of her upper arm.

'Where are you going?'

'I need… I need to wash,' she said, heat climbing into her cheeks as she became all too aware of the sticky residue of their lovemaking between her thighs.

He hadn't used a condom. And she hadn't asked him to.

She dismissed the new ripple of panic. She couldn't think about any consequences now. She'd deal with those later. First, she had to get away from that assessing, intense gaze. And regroup, rethink, re-evaluate her position—her thoughts were so tangled now she could hardly breathe, let alone think.

Could she still stay here? Did she deserve to live in Pierre's home after sleeping with his enemy? But how could she not when she was the only thing standing between La Maison de la Lune and destruction?

She tugged her arm but Maxim held on, his thumb stroking the inside of her elbow and making the prickle of renewed desire distress her even more.

'Please, I need to...' she began.

'Let me help you clean up.' He sat up, swung his long legs to the floor and stood in one smooth move, still keeping a firm grip on her arm.

While she was frantic and awash with guilt, he seemed composed and unperturbed by what had just happened. Her panic increased.

'What?' she asked, the blush burning her cheeks as she tried to avoid looking at his nakedness and deny the melting sensation in her chest—and her sex—at the abrupt but painfully intimate offer to help her wash herself.

How could her body still want him when everything they'd just done was wrong? On so many levels. She'd never really considered her virginity of particular importance. But if that were the case, why had she held onto it for so long? And how had this man been able to destroy all her fears about intimacy so easily—and so quickly?

He tugged her off the bed until she was standing in front of him, then cradled her cheek in his palm. 'Did I hurt you, Cara?'

She shook her head, but the gruff question had the tears she couldn't shed burning the back of her throat. She swallowed hard.

Don't cry, don't you dare cry. It doesn't mean anything. It happened and now it's over and it was a massive mistake.

Her chest felt as if it were imploding.

Not a mistake, an aberration. Brought about by stress, and chemistry. And incredible stupidity.

He doesn't care about you. All he cares about are the vines. And his feud with Pierre. And you don't care about him. Not really. You don't even know him. Your loyalty is to La Maison now. It has to be.

Just because he was Pierre's son. And Pierre had neglected him. He was powerful and successful now. And he'd slept with hundreds of women.

Just because he was your first, it doesn't make this special. First is just a number.

He planned to destroy La Maison, and she couldn't let that happen. That made them enemies, no matter what had just happened in her bed.

'Really, I need to…' She couldn't seem to find

the words, so ashamed now she could hardly talk. She should ask him to leave, but she was so shaky, so confused, she couldn't seem to say anything.

'Breathe, Cara,' he said, taking control, just as he had before.

He threaded his fingers through hers and led her into the bedroom's small and spartan en suite bathroom. Snagging the robe she kept hooked on the door, he handed it to her. She shrugged it on, pathetically grateful for the layer of protection. And even more grateful when he lifted a towel from the pile she kept by the sink and hooked it around his waist.

He slapped down the toilet seat. 'Sit.'

She perched on the seat, trying to focus, trying to find her equilibrium again. But all she seemed capable of doing was gazing at him, mesmerised by his assured, efficient movements.

If he'd made La Maison's reception room look small he made her bathroom look minuscule. Finding soap and a flannel, he ran water into the sink until it was warm, then soaked and lathered the washcloth.

He squatted in front of her and drew apart the robe to expose her tightly closed legs. His gaze met hers as he placed a warm hand on her knee.

'Open for me, Cara,' he murmured, the husky words reminding her of a similar demand earlier, which she had obeyed without question.

'I can… I can do it,' she said, stuttering, her blush radioactive as she reached for the flannel.

'I would like to,' he said. 'I want to be sure I did not hurt you.'

It wasn't a demand, she could have refused him, but the yearning in her chest had her dropping her hand. And allowing him to ease her knees apart.

He washed her gently, carefully, wiping away the evidence of her innocence and their lovemaking with a tender efficiency that stole her breath and had the hollow yearning sinking deep into her abdomen. Her thighs trembled, the renewed pulse of desire impossible to disguise. He touched his thumb to the reddened skin on her hip where he had gripped her in the heat of passion.

'I have bruised you, *ma petite*,' he murmured, sounding genuinely contrite.

'It's okay,' she said. 'It doesn't hurt.'

To her surprise, despite her denial, he leant forward and placed a kiss on the spot. 'You must accept my apologies,' he murmured, his eyes shadowed.

She nodded.

Dumping the flannel in the sink, he pressed her knees back together and smoothed the robe over her nakedness before meeting her eyes. The rueful smile which twisted his lips made her heart beat in an erratic tattoo.

'As much as I would enjoy taking you back to bed, I do not wish to hurt you again.'

'You didn't hurt…'

He touched his finger to her lips, halting her denial. 'Don't lie, Cara, there are enough lies between us already.'

She stared at her hands clasped in her lap, and nodded. 'I know.'

What was wrong with her? One act of tenderness and she was ready to throw herself at him again, even though she knew it was wrong. Exactly how desperate for affection was she?

Tucking a knuckle under her chin, he raised her gaze back to his. 'Now you must tell me why you were untouched.'

'I…' She let out a tense breath. 'Pierre and I didn't have that kind of marriage,' she managed.

He straightened from his crouched position and let out a harsh laugh, the look in his golden eyes not so much suspicious as unconvinced.

'There is only one kind of marriage, Cara. One where a husband takes his wife to his bed.' His gaze roamed over her. 'If you were mine I would not let you out of my bed for a week after we were wed.'

The blush burned her neck and spread across her collarbone, the hunger in his words so compelling it made the hot spot between her thighs throb.

She scrubbed her hand over her cheeks, hoping to calm the colour as she looked away. The sight of his naked chest and the red score marks on his shoulder—which she must have made with her nails—was not helping with her breathing difficulties.

'Pierre was an old man,' she said. 'He wasn't capable of...' Her throat seized. 'Even if I had been willing,' she continued. 'We were just friends. He wanted to marry me so he could give me some security when he was gone, that was what he said.' She didn't tell Durand about the wages Pierre owed her because it would just make her feel more pathetic and expose her marriage to even more of this man's contempt. 'It was never a sexual relationship.'

Maxim stared at the riot of blonde curls, fighting against the desire still pulsing in his groin and the strange wave of elation.

Even if I had been willing.

So she hadn't ever contemplated sleeping with his father. That was good to know.

But then his disgust with the man returned.

He wished Pierre de la Mare wasn't dead, so he could murder the bastard himself.

De la Mare had used Cara Evans to get his revenge against him. But Maxim very much doubted his father's decision to marry this girl had just been about the vineyard, as she clearly believed. The bastard had always had an eye for women, claiming this young beautiful woman as his wife had probably given him some kind of sick ego boost—even if he had never been capable of consummating the relationship.

A sick ego boost that left Maxim with a problem.

He had always planned to raze La Maison to the ground as soon as he purchased the property. It was what he had told de la Mare he would do, all part of the promise he had made to the boy he'd been—an important part of his final revenge for the cruel slights that child had endured.

But how could he in all conscience kick this girl out of her home? Wouldn't that make him as much of a bastard as his father? Especially after he had just taken her innocence?

Not only that, but he hadn't used protection. Something he'd become brutally aware of as he'd cleaned her up.

He frowned. What the hell had possessed him? He hadn't even thought about it. He'd never been that impulsive or reckless before in his life, even as a teenager. Not only did he have no desire to become an accidental parent, but he knew precisely what it was like to be that accidental child. Unwanted, unloved, unimportant. Even now a child could be growing inside her because of his thoughtless behaviour.

The irony of the situation was so apparent it was almost funny. That he should impregnate his own father's widow with an unwanted child—and thereby repeat the old man's crimes.

Except he wasn't laughing. Nothing about this predicament was amusing.

'Are you using contraception, Cara?' he asked, surprised at his ambivalence when her head jerked up, and he deemed the answer from the abject misery on her face.

She shook her head.

'When did you last have a period?'

Embarrassment scorched her cheeks, which would almost have been charming if the possible consequences of their foolishness weren't so dire. 'A few days ago.'

He nodded. 'Then at least we are not in the middle of your cycle.'

There was still a chance their recklessness would have a far higher price than either of them was willing to pay, however. And there was only one solution that he could see which would ensure that didn't happen.

He would take Cara Evans as his mistress. That way, they could arrange for her to take the necessary precautions now to prevent an unwanted pregnancy and he could offer her a place to live while he demolished La Maison—at Château Durand.

Strangely, the thought of supporting Cara and inviting her to live in his home didn't make him as uncomfortable as he would have expected. He had never invited a woman before her to share any of his homes. And he'd never taken a mistress. Up until now, he had always kept his dating habits casual.

He had a business to run. He didn't have time for romance. And he saw no benefit in long-term commitments of any kind. But Cara, for a number of reasons, was different.

Not only did he need to ensure there was no pregnancy, and find her an alternative home, to finally break the last of her ties to his father—but she was the first virgin he had ever slept with, and they shared an insane chemistry which he could see no good reason not to indulge, once all the other issues between them had been resolved. It made sense therefore to have her live at Château Durand and—once this insane chemistry had run its course—he would give her the pay-off he had already offered her.

She had been reluctant to take his money earlier, because she wanted to stay at La Maison, but surely she could see her marriage to his father would never hold up in a court of law now he knew what a sham it had been?

'If there's a…' She sighed. 'If there's a consequence, I can take care of it,' she said, her voice unsteady.

She didn't look him in the eye, and he found his usual cynicism returning. However innocent she might appear, he was not about to trust any woman to 'take care' of the consequences, as she had so coyly put it.

He was a wealthy man and, although she had been unaware of his father's true motives for suggesting marriage, the fact remained she had already married one man she didn't love. What if she were setting her sights on trapping him into marriage too?

Weirdly, the prospect didn't appal him quite as much as it should. But he suspected his magnanimity would disappear once the afterglow still washing through his system had subsided.

'If there are consequences, it is as much my responsibility as yours,' he said, broaching no argument. 'I think the best solution is for you to live at Château Durand. I can arrange for a doctor to attend you as soon as possible to ensure no pregnancy occurs.'

Her head rose, her blue eyes so luminous anticipation surged in his chest.

The truth was, she would make him an excellent mistress. Not only was she exquisite, and surprisingly forthright, but he couldn't remember ever wanting a woman this much. Just thinking of all the things he could teach her, all the pleasure they could share while he did, was making the blood pound straight back into his groin.

But then she said the most ridiculous thing.

'You're offering me a job? As a housekeeper?' she said, sounding wary but hopeful. 'That's… That's amazing and it could solve our problems,' she continued, her voice eager with hope now as he struggled to get his head around her misconception. What had he said to give her the impression he was planning to employ her? 'I'd be happy to give up my right to the de la Mare estate, if you'd just reconsider your plans to demolish La Maison? I know you need the land, but there must be a way to save…'

'I am not offering you a job, and my plans for La Maison will not change.' He interrupted the frantic flow of excited words, allowing his impatience to show. 'I have no need of a housekeeper,' he added, gentling his voice as he watched the hope in her eyes die—and suddenly felt as if he had kicked a kitten. 'And you do not need a job as you will have a generous allowance.'

'But… But what exactly would you be paying me for if I'm not working for you?' she asked, sounding confused.

He frowned. This was ridiculous, she could not be this naïve? Surely.

'Cara,' he said with a sigh, dialling down his impatience—her cluelessness was quite captivating in its own way. And another thing that made her unique. 'I would not be paying you for anything, I would simply be supporting you while you are my mistress.'

CHAPTER SIX

'YOUR...*MISTRESS*?' THE WORD came out on a horrified gasp as Cara struggled to contain her shock, not just at Maxim Durand's bold offer but the pragmatic way in which he delivered it. As if it were perfectly rational to offer to pay a—how had he put it?—'generous allowance' to a woman he was sleeping with.

Perhaps it *was* perfectly rational in the world in which Maxim Durand lived.

What did she know of that world? A world of lavish parties and show-stopping events, of elegant balls and expensive soirées, held on enormous super yachts on the Côte d'Azur or grand hotels on London's Strand or picture-perfect white-sand beaches in the Bahamas. All she'd ever done was read about Maxim Durand's extravagant world in magazines. Perhaps the women he dated—the glamorous supermodels and actresses, the sophisticated hostesses and smart, stunning career women she'd seen on his arm at those events in those same magazines—*didn't* think there was anything amiss with expecting Durand to foot the bill. And maybe there wasn't, *for them*. Because they had money and status and agency too. They would never be dependent on his largesse because they belonged in his rarefied world and knew how it worked. And if they'd ever been powerless, they certainly weren't powerless any more.

But for someone like her, who had fought for every scrap of dignity and respect, and against people's low opinions for most of her life, how could she not be compromised by such an arrangement? Not just compromised but owned. Because without a job, with no way of paying her own way, she would be not just completely dependent on him but little more than his property.

'Yes,' he replied, his puzzled frown only making her feel more compromised, more undermined. '*Ma maîtresse*… Is mistress not the correct word for this in English?' he added.

'I… Yes, but I can't… I don't want to be your mistress,' she said, feeling desperately exposed, and even more ashamed than she had when she'd been lying naked under him, with the orgasms he'd given her still echoing in her sex.

'Why not?' He seemed genuinely confused.

Couldn't he see how belittling, even insulting such a suggestion was? Especially given the names he had called her earlier.

Downstairs, he had accused her of being a whore and a slut. She'd dismissed those insults, once she'd figured out his connection to Pierre and why he was so determined to own the de la Mare vines. Those cruel words had been said in the heat of the moment, while he was processing the reality that his father had rejected him again, even from beyond the grave. And if there was anything Cara understood it was how that kind of rejection made you feel—insignificant, angry, vulnerable, hurt—because she'd felt every one of those emotions herself as a child, when she'd waited for her father to visit her, or to at least call, until she'd finally figured out what his silence meant... That the promises he'd made to her on the steps of the Westminster children's centre had all been convenient lies to get her to go with 'the nice lady' without a fuss.

But the names Maxim had called her haunted her now. Was that what he really thought of her?

'We have a rare chemistry, Cara. We would be foolish not to enjoy it while it lasts.'

Taking her hand, he tugged her off the toilet seat. Wrapping his arm around her waist, he pressed his lips to her neck. She shuddered with a need she couldn't disguise, but found the strength this time to place her hands on his bare chest and push him back.

'Maxim, please don't,' she said.

He let her go but then he smiled, the twist of his lips as cynical as it was amused. 'Why not? When I can smell how much you still want me?'

She tightened the belt on her robe, aware of her nakedness beneath it, and his nakedness beneath the towel—and the ease with which he could turn her own body against her.

But she didn't just feel hurt and insulted now, and compromised, she felt foolish. He was laughing at her naïveté. She got that. She *had* been naïve—to fall into bed with him without a thought to the consequences, and to give him her virginity without realising how much power that would give him. She had also been foolishly optimistic a moment ago, probably because she had been scared and desperate after what she'd done. Foolish to think the solution to a situation which had been decades in the making could ever be solved by him offering her a job.

'I think you should leave,' she managed, straightening her spine and welcoming the spike of anger because it helped steady her nerves.

His smile died. 'What foolishness is this, Cara?'

It hurt to hear him say her name with such gruff intimacy, the desire still thick in his voice.

Because a part of her wanted to sink into that intimacy, to take anything he wanted to offer her. But she knew from grim experience there was always a catch to taking that easy road. And if this evening had taught her one thing it was that instant gratification was not the answer.

He lifted his palm to her cheek but she jerked her head out of his reach. 'Please, Maxim,' she said. 'I need to think.'

'What is there to think about?' he said. 'You are mine now, you need medical attention and a new home. This is the best solution.'

A spark of anger burned under her breastbone. 'The best solution for you, you mean.' The flush rose into her cheeks but she'd be damned if she'd be embarrassed about it. She wasn't the only one who had given in to their desires. 'I don't want to be your...your kept woman.'

'What is this ridiculous term?' he said. 'Kept woman? What does that even mean?'

'It means you'd own me.'

'I would support you—not own you,' he said through gritted teeth, clearly holding onto his temper with an effort. 'You would live at Château Durand, but you would be free to leave whenever you wished.'

'But *this* is my home, Maxim, and I don't want to leave it,' she said, trying to make him understand. If he couldn't see that him supporting her was the same as him owning her, maybe he would understand this. 'And I don't want to let you destroy it, just because you can. I realise your situation with Pierre was complicated, but he left La Maison to me. You can have the vines, there must be a way to get past Pierre's will there. But I owe it to him not to let you destroy his home.'

She'd said the wrong thing, she knew it as soon as she mentioned Pierre's name. Maxim's expression became stormy, but what disturbed her more was the steely determination in his eyes.

'You owe that bastard nothing. He used you to get to me, if you cannot see this you are even more naïve than the evidence suggests. And I will not change my mind about La Maison. I told him I would destroy this place as soon as he was cold in his grave and I will.'

'You…you told him?' Shock came first. '*When* did you tell him?' she asked, her voice thick with horror as a sickening understanding of what was really going on here took root. Maxim's determination to destroy La Maison had nothing to do with his business and everything to do with his need for revenge against a dead man.

'Years ago,' he said dismissively.

'How many years ago?' she asked, the horrifying truth becoming a knot of anguish in her stomach. Had Maxim seduced her deliberately? Had the heat that had flared between them even been real? Or had sleeping with her, in Pierre's house, only hours after his funeral been just another way for Maxim to get revenge against the man who had rejected and exploited him? Had she been used, not just by Pierre but also by his son? 'Was it ten years ago? Five? Two?'

'Why does this matter?' he snapped, the cold steel in his voice a far cry from the furious heat in his eyes. 'You gave your virginity to me. Any loyalty you had to him means nothing now.'

'This isn't about my loyalty to Pierre,' she said, feeling broken inside. Why had she trusted him? A man she barely knew. A man who didn't care about her, had never even pretended to care about her. She'd believed they had some connection, through shared pain, but had that just been a convenient excuse to feed the hunger, and take what her body desired without having to pay the price of her foolishness? 'It's about your need for revenge,' she finished.

'This whole conversation is madness,' he said. 'Pierre is dead. You need a new place to live because La Maison will soon be gone—which means you must grow up and stop talking nonsense.'

Before she could even process the possessive, dictatorial response, he stalked out of the bathroom and flung off the towel.

He dressed as she stood shaking in the doorway.

Leaving his shirt unbuttoned, he returned to her and captured her cheek in his hand. He pressed a kiss to her lips, delved deep with his tongue and her traitorous mouth opened instinctively, her treacherous body melting against his, even as her palms flattened against his abdominal muscles, trying to find the strength to resist him.

When he finally released her from the erotic spell they were both panting, her rigid nipples poking against the silk of her robe, begging for his attention.

'Your body knows you belong to me, even if you do not.' He rubbed his thumb across one nipple, making the brutal sensations dart down to her core. 'When you are ready to face reality I will be waiting,' he added softly, belying the anger she could feel reverberating through his body.

She stood transfixed as she listened to his footsteps disappear down the hallway.

The front door slammed below and she crossed to the window, her limbs still shaky, to see him climb into his SUV. He didn't look up, the headlights illuminating the ancient vines as he backed the car out of the yard in a squeal of rubber.

His clipped parting words echoed in her head as the roar of the SUV's engine disappeared into the night.

Your body knows you belong to me.

Not a threat but a promise. And one she couldn't deny.

She had thrown herself into the wolf's den but, unlike Little Red, she wasn't sure she was smart enough or strong enough to get out again before Maxim Durand devoured her.

CHAPTER SEVEN

Madame de la Mare, there has been a significant development in the settling of your husband's estate. May I come to La Maison this morning to discuss the situation?

CARA WOKE TO find the message from Marcel on her phone. She typed out a reply, telling him she would be ready to see him in half an hour, shocked to realise it was past ten o'clock in the morning.

She dragged her aching body out of bed. She'd had a fitful night's sleep, every one of her dreams—so hot and febrile—haunted by her overwhelming encounter with Maxim Durand.

Opening the shutters of the bedroom she'd moved into after Maxim had stormed out, she allowed her tired eyes to adjust to the morning sunlight and then breathed in a fortifying lungful of the September air. It didn't help.

She squeezed her thighs together to ease the pulse of tenderness.

After a long hot shower, in a vain attempt to clear her groggy thoughts and understand the shameful echo of desire that still lingered, she dressed in her usual outfit of shorts and a T-shirt. Returning to her own bedroom, she stripped the sheets from the bed, careful to avoid looking at the spots of blood left by the innocence she'd lost—not lost, thrown away. She carried the sheets downstairs to the laundry room and stuffed them into the ancient washer.

She turned it on and listened to the old motor whirr into action.

If only she could wash away her stupidity—and the memories of her forbidden night with Maxim—as easily.

Was it her imagination or could she still smell Maxim's scent—sandalwood and salt—lingering on her freshly washed skin?

She needed coffee, and lots of it, before she faced Pierre's lawyer. The last thing she wanted was for Marcel to figure out what she'd done last night.

She was still struggling to pull herself together, sipping her second cup of coffee, when she heard Marcel's car in the driveway. He'd arrived five minutes early.

A thread of unease worked its way into her

stomach as she considered his text again. She'd assumed this was some kind of formality. But why was he eager to see her so early?

The argument with Maxim tormented her as she walked down the hallway to answer Marcel's knock.

Had Maxim taken legal action to dispute Pierre's will already? She supposed she should have anticipated this, but after last night… She'd had some vague hope he would wait, to find a compromise with her.

While the thought of seeing him again wasn't doing anything to alleviate the knots in her belly, it felt better than the wave of foreboding that hit her as she opened the door and saw Marcel's expression.

This was no formality.

'Madame de la Mare, there is a problem with the will,' he said. 'This morning Maxim Durand's legal team have made some outrageous claims which we must dispute immediately. May I come in?'

'Yes, yes, of course.' She held the door open. But her mind couldn't seem to engage with what this all meant as she followed Marcel into the kitchen. It was almost like being in a bad dream as she poured the lawyer a cup of coffee and he set his briefcase down on the kitchen table.

'What claims?' she murmured, but the horrifying reality of what Maxim might have done was already making her stomach hurt.

'Durand has sworn an affidavit that you and he had sexual relations last night and in the process he discovered you were a virgin.' Colour stained the usually staid lawyer's cheeks, the outrage in his voice making the knots in Cara's belly tighten, her mind struggling to comprehend what Marcel was saying.

Maxim had told his legal team she was a virgin, but why would he do that?

She didn't have to wait long to get the answer as Marcel continued in a furious rush.

'Durand's team are looking to have the marriage annulled on the grounds it was never consummated. Of course, this is not a precedent in French law, the marriage does not have to be consummated for it to be legal, but as he is trying to assert that you were *never* in an intimate relationship with your husband, even before your marriage, this might have some weight with the court. But what is more outrageous, his legal team have released a press statement detailing Durand's claims against you, no doubt to force your hand and get us to withdraw to avoid further scandal. It is only a matter of time before the press turn up here. Maxim Durand is a...' The usually congenial Marcel bit off the swear word she suspected was about to come out of his mouth. 'Our path is clear, we must counter the man's lies immediately with a written affidavit from you disputing these claims which we will also release to the press, showing the whole region what... How do you say it in English? What *trash* he really is.'

Marcel finished with a flourish, his hazelnut-brown eyes full of fighting spirit.

Cara's knees gave way and the coffee cup dropped to the floor, but the crash of breaking porcelain was muffled by the deafening punches of her heartbeat.

The harsh reality of what Maxim had done began to seep into her bones like a virus, both debilitating and unbearably painful. This was all her own fault, for thinking she could take on a wolf, and survive.

She hadn't just been foolish and naïve, she'd been a fantasist. She'd realised last night how much Maxim hated his father, but she hadn't believed he would be this cruel, this callous. That he would be prepared to destroy her reputation as well as her home, simply to exact his revenge.

She sniffed as the tears she'd refused to shed last night slipped over her lids.

'*Madame*, do not despair,' Marcel said, sitting next to her and resting a paternal hand over hers on the table. 'We will dispute his claims. In truth, he may have given us a tactical advantage; telling such lies means we can make a counterclaim for defamation.'

'But we can't,' she murmured, scrubbing the pointless tears off her cheeks and forcing herself to meet the lawyer's trusting gaze. 'Because everything he said is true.'

'Maxim, is that your communications guy?' Victor Dupont, Maxim's estate manager, said in French, clearly amused. 'What is he doing here, where the real work takes place?'

Maxim glanced up from tying off the twine on the new vines he and Victor had been inspecting all day—well used to Victor's scathing opinion of the marketing end of winemaking.

He squinted into the sun, wiping the sweat off his forehead. 'I think so,' he murmured. Victor was right to be amused, Rick Carson looked incongruous in his designer suit, picking his way through the rows of vines.

Spending the day out in the fields had seemed like a good way to sweat away his concerns over the Cara Evans situation—and the lingering desire that would not die—not to mention his discomfort at the move he'd been forced to make this morning.

He'd rung his legal team early, after spending the night figuring out a solution to Cara's stubborn refusal to even consider his offer.

The affidavit he'd signed about their night together had made him uncomfortable; it was ruthless, but he'd done ruthless things before to get what he wanted, and she had left him with no choice. He needed to break her misguided loyalty to de la Mare. And because of the problem of a possible pregnancy, he did not have time to do this gently. He wanted her safely installed at Château Durand and the purchase of de la Mare's estate set in motion before he left France next week for his vineyards in California. By the time he returned, she would be over her stubbornness and ready to see the benefits of becoming his mistress.

The truth was he had lost his temper last night when she had mentioned his father. Blindsided by a surge of possessiveness... And, yes, dammit, jealousy. Which didn't make a lot of sense. But then very little about his reactions to Cara made sense.

After spending a sleepless night thinking about the way she had come apart in his arms, he had come to several important conclusions, however. He had no need to be jealous of his father. Not only was the man dead, but Cara had never given herself to him, only to Maxim. Perhaps he had also been too hasty insisting that La Maison be demolished. He had made that threat to de la Mare because he had been furious when the man had dared to ask him for his help, attempting to play on Maxim's sentiment for a place he had never been allowed to even step inside. But his goal when returning to Burgundy had always been to create his own legacy and make wines that were better than de la Mare's had ever been. Owning the vines he had sweated over as a child was enough. If Cara was willing to come and live at Château Durand, perhaps he could be magnanimous about the house?

By the time Carson reached him and Victor, he was sweating profusely. 'Maxim, why don't you ever answer your cell phone?' he said in his broad Californian accent.

Maxim shrugged. 'I don't have it with me,' he replied. He'd left his phone in the car. The whole purpose had been to get back to basics today. And get away from the endless thoughts of Cara.

'What is the problem?' he asked, because there was obviously a problem or Carson wouldn't have risked ruining his two-thousand-dollar shoes.

'We need you back at headquarters. The internet has blown up. We've got local news reporters doorstepping the office and the story's threatening to spread to the nationals.'

'What story?' Maxim snapped, annoyed now as well as confused. He did not appreciate getting dressed down by a subordinate.

'The one your legal team broke at nine thirty

this morning…' Carson paused to take a breath. 'The one in which you question the validity of Pierre de la Mare's recent marriage, thanks to your seduction of Madame de la Mare last night.'

'*C'est quoi ça?*' Maxim's shout rang across the fields, the trickle of irritation turning into a flood of volcanic rage. 'I never sanctioned such a thing.'

Someone at Brocard et Fils, his solicitors, had released the details of the affidavit he'd signed this morning to the press? The lava rose up his chest like a fire-breathing dragon, threatening to blow his head off. He threw the last of the twine to Victor, who caught it one-handed. 'Finish this, Victor. I must go.'

The estate manager nodded.

Maxim stalked across the fields towards his vehicle, his fury building with every step.

'But if you didn't sanction it, who did?' Carson asked, running to keep up with his long strides.

'I don't know but I will find out,' he snarled through gritted teeth.

Reaching the SUV, he jumped into the driver's side, the fury firing through his veins at the imbecile who had done this—but right behind it was the dread making his stomach heave towards his throat.

Cara.

As uncomfortable as he had been taking the nuclear option to make her see the reality of her position, and his, he had never intended to publicly humiliate her. And having the details of their first night together—details he had given in confidence to his attorney—become the subject of a media storm would do exactly that.

He had seen the shame in her eyes last night as she sat in the bathroom. Shame which made no sense. She had been innocent. In fact, the chemistry between them had been so strong, neither one of them would have been able to deny it for long. What had happened was inevitable. And it had been good, for both of them. Very good, despite her inexperience. So good he hadn't been able to stop thinking of having her in his bed again.

His fingers flexed on the steering wheel.

Was that the real reason he had taken action this morning to force her hand? Not because he wanted to ensure no pregnancy occurred from their night together, but because he wanted her?

He shook off the thought as he hunted for the car keys in the glovebox.

No, that was madness. However much he might want her, it was only sexual desire. And sexual desire always died.

But as he jammed his keys into the SUV's transmission, the memory of Cara's wary expression the night before clouded his vision. He could picture her now, her hands clasped in her lap while he washed her as gently as he could, and examined the red skin where he had bruised her during their furious coupling. And for the first time in a long time his stomach dropped, and his heart rammed his throat.

He recognised the feeling as the same one that had pursued him for years after he'd left Burgundy. Guilt.

He turned on the ignition, swung his head round to start backing down the track, and hit the gas.

Carson jumped back as the dirt sprayed his suit and the SUV lurched into reverse.

Maxim swung the vehicle round and sped down the track, heading for the back road that led through his property towards de la Mare's estate.

Towards La Maison de la Lune.

And mentally prepared himself to do something he hadn't done since the morning he had told his mother he was leaving Burgundy…

Apologise to a woman.

He arrived at La Maison ten minutes later, to find a local news crew outside that looked to be in the process of packing up their equipment.

As soon as he stepped out of the car, the reporter rushed towards him with a microphone in her fist, the cameraman not far behind. She shoved the microphone in his face, firing a string of questions at him about his scandalous 'tryst' with Madame de la Mare.

'*Sans commentaires*,' he snapped, brushing them aside before pounding on the door of the farmhouse. 'Cara, open the door. I need to speak to you.'

After five agonising minutes the door opened, and Marcel Caron glared at him.

'You? What are you doing here? Haven't you caused enough...'

'*Tais-toi!*' He cut the lawyer's diatribe off, then barged past him to slam the door shut. 'I have no wish to give those parasites more to talk about,' he continued in English, just in case the bastards could record them through the door.

'I find your sudden discretion hard to believe,' the lawyer sneered back, keeping the conversation in English. 'Given the damage you have already...'

'Where's Cara?' he demanded as he stalked past the lawyer. He didn't have time for the guy's micro-aggressions.

He reached the reception room and was immediately struck by the sense of emptiness which lingered over the room that hadn't been there the night before. Where was the warmth, the touches of personality and hospitality he had noticed yesterday when he had walked in here? The spray of wild flowers in a glass jar on the mantel? The scent of rosemary and lavender? The erotic aroma of Cara herself which had invaded his senses and driven him wild?

'Cara?' he shouted again, the hollow ache tangling with the heavy weight of foreboding which sat in his stomach. 'Stop hiding, we need to talk.'

'She is gone,' the lawyer interrupted softly, the bitter accusation in his voice replaced with weariness. 'She left this morning before the media hounds arrived, thank God.'

Maxim swung round. 'Where did she go?'

'I do not know,' the man said, then lifted a sheaf of official-looking papers from the briefcase he had open on the table. 'But she left you these.'

Maxim frowned down at the papers and shoved his hands into his pockets. He didn't want to take them, whatever they were.

Cara had left? Without contacting him? Without giving him a chance to explain?

'Take them,' Marcel said, the edge of accusation returning. 'It's what you wanted.'

The harsh stab of regret dug into Maxim's stomach. Whatever those papers contained, this was not the outcome he had planned.

What if he could never hold her again? Hear her sighs? Her sobs? Feel her body close around his?

What surprised him, though, was the realisation that it wasn't just the chance to have her back in his bed that he regretted the most.

What if he never saw her face again? So open, so trusting, the flags of colour on her cheeks when she was aroused? What if he never heard her voice again either? Crisp and smoky, arousing him and antagonising him at one and the same time…

Caron dumped the papers onto the table. The thud yanked Maxim out of the unfamiliar reverie. The lawyer let out a hefty sigh. 'She has relinquished any claim on the de la Mare estate and this property. I will file the papers with the court tomorrow morning and the estate will be put up for auction to pay the debts very soon.' The lawyer's gaze met his, the accusation back full force. 'I realise you are a ruthless man, but I never realised you were this ruthless.'

He could refute the man's claims. He hadn't intended for the affidavit to become public, certainly hadn't planned for it to be leaked to the press. And he hadn't seduced Cara with any ulterior motive. But he didn't really care what Marcel Caron thought of him. The threat of public or private censure had never stopped him from doing what he had to do to grow his business, and destroy his rivals, before now.

Which only made the numbness spreading through his body all the more confusing, and unexplainable. How was it that he found he did care what Cara thought of him?

'Here—' the lawyer lifted a sealed envelope with his name written on it in neat black lettering '—she left you this too.'

He snatched the envelope from the man's hand and ripped it open.

Maxim,
  I realise what happened last night was simply a means to an end for you—and it was naïve of me to think it was anything else.
  I hope you can be at peace with your father now.
  Goodbye,
  Cara Evans

He let the paper drop, then thrust his fingers through his hair. His guts churned as the numbness was replaced with anger. Not just with himself, but with Cara.

Did she think he'd planned this? That he'd seduced her to get hold of the estate? That he would stoop so low as to use his body to further his business ambitions? Did she think what had happened between them hadn't been as spontaneous for him as it had been for her?

She'd run without listening to his side, without giving him a chance to explain, but, worse than that, she had folded her hand because of what? A few press enquiries?

Yes, his legal team had made a catastrophic error, and heads would soon be rolling because of it, but why hadn't she stayed to fight this thing? Why had she given up so easily?

And that nonsense at the end of the letter about his father. He didn't give a damn about that old bastard. He'd moved on from that rejection a long time ago. Why hadn't she believed him?

'You need to tell me where she's gone,' he demanded, focusing his rising fury on the only person there. He needed to find her, to get her back. To get rid of this growing emptiness inside.

'I told you, I have no idea,' Marcel said.

Although Maxim suspected the other man wouldn't have told him where she'd gone even if he knew, he also suspected he wasn't lying.

'I'm not even sure she knew,' Caron added wearily. 'It took all of my powers of persuasion to get her to take a few hundred euros so she could buy a train ticket and survive until she finds a new job.'

'She has no money?' Maxim asked, his fury building. 'How can she have no money? Was she not working for de la Mare? Surely she must have saved something?' From what he could see of La Maison, for all the homely charms she had added to the place, she and de la Mare had been living very frugally.

'Pierre hadn't paid her for months,' Marcel announced, and Maxim's temper shot into the stratosphere. 'That's how he persuaded her to marry him,' Marcel added. 'Apparently he told her he would be able to leave her the money he owed her in his will from his pension, if she were his widow. If I had known this before now I would have told her: there was no pension.'

'That bastard.' Maxim stalked back towards the farmhouse entrance. The surge of guilt wasn't helping to contain his rising fury at Cara's foolish actions.

His father had always been a bastard. So it was no surprise the conniving cheapskate had found a way to cheat his housekeeper out of her wages before he died. And trick her into marriage in a pathetic last-ditch attempt to stop Maxim owning the de la Mare legacy.

But if Cara was destitute, why hadn't she accepted Maxim's offer? And why had she capitulated so easily over the will? Surely this was madness.

He understood pride, but you couldn't eat pride, and it didn't put a roof over your head. Was the thought of becoming his mistress really so repugnant that she would rather starve?

He shoved past the waiting reporters, ignoring the lights flashing in his face and the probing questions being shouted at him. Not to mention the hit to his ego at Cara's foolish decision to run, rather than accept his help.

He tugged his cell phone out of his pocket and started dialling. Once he'd climbed into the SUV, he stuck the phone on hands-free and began issuing orders while he reversed out of the yard.

He needed Cara Evans found.

The guilt stabbed into his gut as he drove off the de la Mare property. But more than that was the crippling feeling of loss—that he did not fully understand—and the terrifying sense of *déjà vu*.

His mother's voice echoed in his head… A voice which had haunted his dreams for so many years after her death, a voice he hadn't heard for years.

'Maxim, ne t'en vas pas. Je ne peux pas vivre sans toi.'

Maxim, do not leave. I cannot live without you.

As he accelerated along the country road, he allowed his fury to overwhelm the memories. He would bring Cara back. And make her see reason.

He took the turning to the local train station.

She only had a few hours' start on him—she wouldn't be that hard to find. Especially not with the resources he had at his disposal.

This wasn't over. It couldn't be. He wouldn't let it be. Not like this.

CHAPTER EIGHT

Five months later

'YOU SHOULD SEE the crowd out there tonight. I swear I've spotted more movie stars already than are at my local multiplex.'

'That's cool.' Cara sent a wan smile to her new friend Dora, whose excitement at their latest waitressing gig would have been infectious if only she weren't so exhausted. She eased the zip up on the short black skirt she wore for her waitressing work but left the button at the top undone. But as she donned her white shirt, she encountered another problem. She hunched her shoulders, attempting to hide the way the shirt's buttons threatened to pop out of their holes over her ever-increasing bust.

How much longer was she going to be able to hide her condition? And what would she do when that day came? This job was the only thing keeping her afloat. But working any and every shift she could get was starting to take its toll.

She slammed the locker door and slipped on the four-inch heels the luxury hotel on London's Embankment insisted on, then stretched her back to alleviate the ache which had set in a week ago.

She pressed her palm to the curve of her stomach, and the trickle of panic receded. The wave of love she already felt for the child swept through her and a tired smile edged her lips. This baby was hers, and only hers, something she could love and cherish the way she never had been.

'How far along are you, honey?' Dora murmured.

Cara's head swung round, to find Dora's gaze on her, full of concern and curiosity.

She dropped her hand from her stomach, the panic returning to tighten around her throat. 'I... How did you know?' she managed. Dora was her friend, surely she wouldn't tell their line manager.

'Because you've got that dreamy look on your face I had with my two,' Dora said easily. 'And that bump...' she glanced pointedly at Cara's tummy '...is becoming harder and harder to miss.'

'Is it really that obvious?' Cara whispered, the exhaustion threatening to envelop her. 'I can't... I can't afford to lose any shifts.'

'Isn't there anyone who can help you out, luv?'

Cara shook her head, grateful Dora hadn't asked the obvious question—where is the father?

'I'll pick up all your drinks then. And you can take my canapés, okay, they're lighter.'

'Thank you.' Cara blinked, feeling stupidly emotional at the other woman's kindness.

'You never know, you might find a sugar daddy tonight.' Dora grinned as they made their way up the back stairs of the Regency hotel towards the huge ballroom where the Valentine's Day event they had been hired to work on was taking place. 'There's certainly enough mega-rich men at this thing.'

'I wish,' Cara said, forcing a smile to her lips at the renewed blip of panic, knowing there was one rich man she really did not want to see.

She entered the kitchen from the staff entrance. Surely even she couldn't be that unlucky. And anyway, serving staff like her were all but invisible at these events.

After the kitchen staff loaded up her first tray, she walked into the ballroom.

Chandeliers sparkled, hanging from the room's vaulted ceiling. Towering sprays of roses and lilies were arranged in crystal vases and added a heady aroma to the cloying scent of expensive colognes and fragrances. Conversation hummed over the delicate strains of classical music. Shelves full of leather-bound books lined the walls, a nod to the cavernous room's former life as a historic library. Mullioned windows looked out over the Embankment, framing the spotlit majesty of Big Ben and the purple glow of the Millennium Wheel on the opposite bank. The room was packed with people—men in dinner suits and tuxedos and women in elaborate designer gowns of every conceivable hue, their precious jewels glittering in the low lighting.

Cara's heart fluttered as she absorbed the splendour of the scene and she edged into the crowd to serve the delicate lamb skewers with a tamarind dipping sauce.

She pasted a bright smile on her face. Every one of these people belonged to a world in which Cara would never belong. This was Maxim's world, she thought. Rich, beautiful, arrogant and entitled.

She shifted the weight to her other arm, mindful of the baby bump she had hidden beneath the tray. And willed away the ache in her chest that thoughts of Maxim and their one night together always caused.

She had struggled with the question of whether or not to tell Maxim about the pregnancy when the doctor had confirmed it. She'd tortured herself with all the obvious questions, racked by a guilt she still hadn't quite been able to shake.

Didn't every man deserve to know he was going to be a father?

And didn't every child deserve to know its dad?

Despite his actions later, Maxim had been tender towards her that night, after he'd discovered her virginity. And she knew he could feel deeply from the way he'd reacted to Pierre's will.

But then she thought of her own father, and how easily he had discarded her. And the cruel way Maxim had discarded her too. She knew she'd made the right choice.

These weren't normal circumstances. And Maxim wasn't any normal man. Not only was he rich and powerful, and overwhelming, he had proven how ruthless he could be. He'd also made it very clear he had no desire to become a father.

She kept her head down as she weaved through the opulent crowd, grateful for the cloak of invisibility she wore as one of the waitstaff, and forced her mind back to the job at hand—keeping her elbow braced and her arm steady so she didn't end up spraying tamarind dipping sauce over anyone's designer ballgown before her shift was over...

In six never-ending hours' time.

'Maxim, darling, what are you doing out here? The party's inside!'

Maxim turned from the view of the Thames to find his so-called date, Kristin Delinski, strutting towards him as if she were still on the catwalk, carrying two champagne flutes. Her legs had to be freezing in that short leather skirt, he thought dispassionately, as he took a deep breath of the chilly night air. Air he'd needed as soon as they'd walked into this mayhem twenty minutes ago. Not for the first time, he wondered what had possessed him to attend tonight's event and invite her along. When had he ever celebrated Valentine's Day?

His gaze flickered over his date's expertly made-up face as she handed him one of the glasses. He'd probably had some vague notion of taking her to bed, but the minute she'd climbed into his car he'd known that wasn't going to happen. The sexual spark which had once been there for her, and all the other women he'd dated casually over the years, was gone—blown away by the tornado that had hit his sex life five months ago and still wasn't finished wreaking havoc on his libido.

When was he going to be able to stop obsessing about that one night? A night that had meant nothing.

Cara Evans had vanished. He'd searched for her for months, but every avenue he—and the different investigators he'd hired—had tried had hit a dead end. The woman was a ghost, without a family, any known acquaintances and, most infuriating of all, not even a social media footprint.

'It's Valentine's Night and you never know...' Kristin paused to flutter her heavily painted eyelashes. 'You might get extremely lucky if you make more of an effort.'

'Duly noted,' Maxim murmured as he sipped the champagne—and assessed the vintage. Not as good as Durand's best champagne, but not bad.

The problem was he didn't want to make the effort, because he had no desire whatsoever to get lucky with Kristin, despite her mile-long legs and that provocative self-confidence, which had once made her such an appealing distraction whenever he was in London on a business trip. He could barely even remember those encounters now, because his memory was still full of another woman's sighs, and sobs. Luminous bright blue eyes filled with shame and confusion, soft dewy skin that smelled of wild flowers and arousal, ripe nipples begging for his...

Merde! Stop thinking about her—she's gone; she didn't want you...

Kristin ran a fingernail across his jaw, interrupting his frustrating thoughts. 'Really, Max,' she said, using the nickname he hated as she pouted. 'Are you even listening to me?'

Non.

Just as he opened his mouth to tell her the truth, something caught his eye at the far end of the balcony.

A serving girl in the standard waitressing outfit of white shirt and short black skirt had walked out of the ballroom to offer a tray of canapés to the only other couple on the terrace. Her lush figure was barely contained by the fitted uniform. Desire sizzled along his nerve-endings, the heady fizz of recognition a great deal more intoxicating than the vintage champagne. He grasped Kristin's wrist to pull her hand away from his face so he could get a better look at the waitress.

Was it her? Could it possibly be her? Or was his mind playing tricks on him again?

He'd conjured up this image a dozen times before in the last five months. Fleeting glimpses of Cara's hair, her figure, that heart-shaped face—on the streets of Paris and Rome and even Johannesburg—had stirred his senses, only to destroy him seconds later when he looked closer and realised the woman wasn't her.

But as he studied the apparition this time, instead of dissolving into reality, the yearning became stronger.

The waitress's blonde hair was piled in a haphazard chignon, glowing gold in the flicker of lamplight on the balcony. His fingers tensed on Kristin's wrist as he recalled the silky feel of Cara's hair as the pins scattered across the floor of La Maison and the locks tumbled into his hands.

'Max, what is it?' Kristin's tone was annoyed, but he could barely hear her above the thundering of his own heartbeat. 'Why are you staring at the waitress like that? Do you know her?'

'*Oui*,' he murmured, but he wasn't talking to his date any more as he watched the girl turn and head towards them with her tray.

'*Lève la tête*,' he whispered, willing her to lift her head so he could get a better look at her face. But he already knew, from the sensations charging through his body, making his sex harden and his breathing accelerate. He'd found her. At last.

Just as she had done all those months ago, she obeyed his command instinctively and their gazes locked. She stopped dead. Stunned surprise crossed her face first, followed by panic and guilt, but then her gaze flicked to Kristin and what he saw in her face—could it be envy, hurt, regret?—had adrenaline firing through his system like a drug.

And he had the answer he had been looking for, for five months, without even realising it. She still wanted him too.

The tray clattered to the floor, making everyone but him—and her—jump as the food splattered across the stones. She stood transfixed, her body trembling as if she were in a trance from which she couldn't escape.

Reaching into his pocket, he pulled out his wallet and shoved some notes into Kristin's hand. 'Find your own way home,' he murmured, tucking his wallet back into his jacket pocket, his movements deliberately slow and cautious, his gaze fixed on his runaway lover.

'Well, really, Max, I...'

He tuned out Kristin's indignant response as he walked past her, towards Cara, his gaze devouring every inch of her.

Something about her was different. Her figure? Why did it seem fuller, even more lush than he remembered it? She edged back a step and the lamplight hit her face.

Concern lanced through him.

Where had those dark circles come from, under her eyes? Why did she seem so fragile despite her curves?

The wave of possessiveness and protectiveness, which he'd convinced himself didn't exist, surged up his chest.

'Cara,' he said, her name rough on his tongue as he lifted his hand to beckon her towards him, scared to make any sudden movement in case she vanished and he discovered he had been dreaming all along.

Like a young deer scenting the hunter, she snapped out of her trance and spun round.

He cursed as she shot back into the ballroom.

'Cara, *reviens ici!*' he yelled, demanding she come back, but she'd already disappeared into the throng of guests.

He shoved his way through the crowd after her, not caring about the drinks he spilled, the stern looks and shouted admonishments he received from the people he pushed out of the way. He craned his neck to look over the heads of the other guests. Relief rushed through him as he spotted her golden hair disappearing through a door at the end of the great hall, marked Staff Only.

The crowd parted as he barged past, the relief and adrenaline—and the sharp swell of desire— joined by a rising tide of fury.

This was no dream, it was real. *She* was real.

She'd run from him once. No way was he going to let her run again.

Cara kicked off her shoes as soon as she got through the staff door and picked them up, to race past the wait stations where the other servers were having their trays filled, her exhaustion forgotten in a rush of pure unadulterated panic.

Maxim! Maxim was here and he'd found her.

'Cara, is everything okay?' She shook her head

at Dora's shocked question as she rushed past her friend towards the stairwell to the locker room.

Maxim, who had been with another woman.

Kristin Delinski, a world-renowned supermodel who Cara had recognised instantly from the magazines she'd once loved to read. But had avoided in the last five months.

She swiped away the tear that slipped down her cheek as she made it to the stairs.

Good God, why are you crying? Of course he's with another woman. He's probably had tons of other women since that night, all of them more beautiful and accomplished than you.

Her line manager, Martha Simpson, was coming up the stairs from the staff locker room as she headed down. 'Cara, where are you going? There's two more hours left on your shift!'

'I'm sorry, I've got to go,' she said, then rushed past, not waiting for the woman's answer. She wouldn't be able to come back, not now he knew where she worked.

She made it to the locker room.

He wasn't following her. Why would he? But, even so, urgency made her hands clumsy as she grabbed her bag, shoved the heels inside, slipped on her flats and untied the apron. She was reaching for her coat when she heard footsteps enter the room, and a deep voice had her fingers jerking on the coat.

'Cara…why did you run?'

Hearing the roughened R, the husky intimacy of her name said in his gruff French accent— a sound which had woken her from dreams so many nights since she'd left France—had so many conflicting emotions hurtling into her chest. She turned to face him without thinking, the urge to see him again riding roughshod over all her instincts of self-preservation.

She realised her mistake as his gaze tracked down to her stomach, and the baby bump, which was no longer hidden by the apron.

His eyes met hers, the golden-brown rich with passion and fury and yet dark with accusation, and something she didn't understand—because it looked strangely like hurt.

'The child, is it mine?'

She wanted to say no, to protect herself and her baby from that caustic cynical gaze, and the character of the man she knew lay behind it. Powerful, arrogant, demanding, ruthless. More committed to his revenge against a dead man than he would ever be to someone like her. But something about the flash of pain which had been there and then gone in a heartbeat had the lie catching in her throat.

She turned back to the locker, releasing the coat, and pressed her forehead against the cool metal. The weariness that had haunted her for weeks returned to sap the last of the energy from her limbs, but this time it was accompanied by the bone-sapping guilt she had wrestled with for months. She thought she'd conquered it, thought she'd come to terms with her choice not to contact Maxim. But if she had, why could the truth still punish her?

She placed a hand over her stomach and silently apologised to her child before saying the only words that would come out of her mouth.

'Yes. Yes, it is.'

CHAPTER NINE

MAXIM WAS IN shock. Or at least he thought he was. Because it was hard to tell, so many emotions were bombarding him at once he could hardly control them, let alone differentiate or identify them.

Cara was carrying his child.

The only emotion he knew he didn't feel was regret—that he had found her. For a man who had never intended to become a father this didn't make a lot of sense, but there was no denying the surge of protectiveness that had blindsided him when he'd first identified Cara on the balcony.

'Why did you not contact me?' he demanded, allowing his anger to show—to cover the hurt he didn't want to acknowledge.

She raised her head, the tiredness in her eyes and those dark shadows under them that had disturbed him so much making his fingers clench into fists.

He swallowed hard, forcing himself to resist

the urge to pick her up and cradle her against his chest. She looked as if she were about to collapse. How long had she been working like this, late into the night, constantly on her feet?

'Because I didn't want you to know,' she said.

The pain caused by the softly spoken words arrowed into his gut, making him stiffen.

He stepped forward and grasped her arm. 'You carry my child and you had no intention of telling me? *Ever?*' he said, not quite able to keep the whisper of shocked betrayal out of his voice. Things had ended badly between them, and part of that had been his fault, but he did not deserve this.

She tugged her arm free. 'This is *my* child, Maxim. I chose to have it. You don't have to be a part of this.'

'Are you mad?' His gaze roamed down to her stomach, where the baby grew. 'This is my flesh and blood. Do you really think I would choose to abandon it?'

She looked down, breaking eye contact, but he could hear the distress in her voice when she murmured, 'Men do it all the time.'

He cursed under his breath. 'Not this man,' he said, more frustrated than he had ever been in his life. 'I am not my father, if that is what you believe.' Would he never be free of that bastard's crimes? To be judged now by the sins of his father would almost be laughable if it weren't so unjust.

She glanced up, the guilt in her eyes tempered by the shadow of doubt, and regret. And, although she remained silent, he could hear again what she had said that night.

'This isn't about my loyalty to Pierre... It's about your need for revenge.'

And the question that had tormented him a thousand times since in his nightmares.

If you are really better than him, why did you insist on your revenge, insist on destroying La Maison, when letting her keep the house might have persuaded her to stay?

'I don't want to argue with you,' she said, clasping her arms around her waist in a defensive gesture that had the guilty recriminations receding.

What the hell was she protecting herself against? Him?

Whatever his crimes against her that night, whatever he had done, or failed to do, she had taken the decision not to tell him about his child.

'I deserve a better answer than that,' he said. 'You had no right not to inform me I was going to become a father.'

She lifted her chin, the spark of defiance in her eyes somehow better than the exhaustion, or the guilt, or the regret. 'I didn't think you'd want to know,' she said.

'When did I give you that impression?' he demanded, the fury and frustration threatening to strangle him. 'I asked you to come to Château Durand that night, I offered you my support.'

'While making it very clear you thought a pregnancy would be an inconvenience,' she fired back. 'A problem to be solved...' Her blue eyes darkened with sadness. 'To be taken care of.'

'Because at the time it was,' he barked out, no longer able to contain his anger. She flinched and he forced himself to lower his voice again, to remain calm. Shouting at her was not the answer. 'But the choice would always have been yours.' He ground out the words, annoyed that he had to spell it out. Did she think he was some kind of monster? The kind of man who would have insisted she have an abortion? 'But whatever I said then hardly applies now. The child is now a fact.'

She nodded, the flicker of guilt in her eyes some compensation. 'Okay,' she said.

A part of him was still furious with her, still angry, and still upset that she had run without giving him a chance to explain. A chance to change his mind about the damn house. But the protective side that had surged to life on the balcony... Hell, all those months ago, when he had tended her in the bathroom in La Maison de la Lune, went some way to calming his fury now. He had searched for a glimpse of her for months in every crowd and been unable to forget her, no matter how hard he tried. However shocking the news of her pregnancy was, and however hurtful her decision not to tell him about it, his first priority now had to be to take care of her, and ensure she didn't run from him again.

So he went with instinct and cupped her cheek.

Her head jerked up, but she didn't draw away from his touch as he ran his thumb over her bottom lip.

The surge of desire and the urge to feast on that mouth again was so fierce he had to force himself not to act on it. Giving in to this hunger now was not an option, but he took some consolation from the dazed arousal in her eyes.

'You look exhausted,' he murmured. 'Are you well?'

'I'm just tired. It's been a long night,' she said, the weary resignation in her tone crucifying him. He made no effort to control the shaft of tenderness, of possession that knifed through him this time.

They had a lot of talking to do. And probably arguing too. And he had no clue whatsoever how to handle the news that he was going to become a father, the fact of the child an abstract concept that he would have to deal with another time.

But right now she looked barely strong enough to stand.

Nudging her aside, he took her coat from the locker and wrapped it around her shoulders then lifted her bag out of her hand. 'Come, we will go back to my hotel.'

'It's okay. I live in East London. I can get the Tube home,' she said, reaching for her bag. He whisked it out of her grasp and she frowned. 'If you tell me where you're staying, Maxim, I'll come over tomorrow and we can talk then about the baby.'

He let out a harsh laugh at her earnest expression. 'Do you truly believe I would be so stupid as to let you out of my sight again?'

She didn't say anything, clearly stunned by his question. He couldn't imagine why she would be so surprised. Why would he trust her, after what she had done?

He cupped her elbow and guided her out of the locker room and through the back entrance of the hotel into the street. Her body was limp, her demeanour passive. The fight had drained out of her. He would have been more pleased if his concern for her well-being wasn't starting to gag him. Was it normal for pregnant women to be so fragile?

Yes, it was.

Fear knifed through his gut at the thought of his mother.

He whistled for a passing cab, which skidded to

a stop at the kerb. He helped her in then climbed in behind her, giving the name of his hotel to the driver. It was only a few streets away, but he wasn't taking any chances.

She scooted to the other side of the bench seat, to stare out of the window into the night. He saw her brush a lone tear from her cheek, her face illuminated by the passing cars and the neon signs of the Strand as the cab arrived at their destination, the landmark six-star art deco hotel where he kept a suite whenever he was in town.

He stepped out of the cab and paid the driver, then took her elbow again when she climbed out. He signalled a bellboy.

The teenager shot over. 'Yes, Mr Durand, how can I help you?'

'I need *un obstétricien* to come to my suite immediately. Ask the concierge to contact the hotel doctor to find the best available at this hour. Money is no object,' he said, giving the boy a twenty-pound tip before the kid shot off towards the concierge's desk.

Cara's arm tensed in his as he led her through the lobby to the lifts, but she didn't resist him.

'I already have a doctor, Maxim,' she said, the exhaustion in her voice so apparent now he decided not to resist his instincts any longer. He scooped her into his arms and carried her into the lift, ignoring her efforts to protest.

'*Bien*,' he said, stabbing the button to the penthouse. 'Now you will have two doctors.'

'Your girlfriend is healthy but undernourished, Mr Durand, and exhausted. I've given her a supply of vitamins, but what she needs most right now is rest. And someone to make sure she eats three square meals a day. No more working on her feet for hours would also be a good idea,' the doctor said, giving Maxim a judgemental look.

He ignored it. He didn't care what the obstetrician thought of him, as long as she could reassure him that Cara was well.

The doctor packed the last of her instruments into her bag. 'Your child is certainly much livelier than its mother at the moment. It has a firm, steady heartbeat and quite an impressive kick.'

'It kicks?' he asked, the words catching in his throat as his heart somersaulted in his chest. He'd been trying not to think too much about the baby.

The doctor smiled. 'Your child is very active and big for dates, from what I can tell by touch. Cara says she missed her last prenatal appointment.' The doctor sighed as she snapped the bag closed. 'Apparently she overslept.' The woman shot him the same judgemental look, probably wondering why a man as rich as he was had allowed the mother of his child to work long into the night for the minimum wage.

Maxim tried not to care what the doctor thought of him. Cara would no longer be risking her health working dead-end jobs. She might not have wanted him to support her, but everything had changed. He had a responsibility to her now that he had no intention of shirking, so he was going to give her no choice in the matter.

She was coming to live in Burgundy with him, as soon as he could make arrangements for them to be married. He'd considered the pros and cons of the arrangement while the doctor examined Cara and he could see no other solution that would satisfy him. He couldn't trust her not to risk her health and well-being. And—while he doubted he would ever be capable of having a relationship with this child—he refused to allow it to be born without his name.

The doctor passed him her card. 'If you want to bring her to the clinic tomorrow we can do a proper blood workup and an ultrasound scan to give the baby a thorough check. But, for the moment, I'd suggest leaving her alone to get a good night's sleep.'

The implication was clear in the doctor's stern expression—no sex tonight. Perhaps she had heard of his 'insatiable appetites' from the tabloid press. While he had earned that reputation in the past, the doctor's stern look was ironic now, given that he hadn't had the inclination to touch any other woman since he had left Cara's bed five months ago.

'Do not worry, I have no intention of demanding any sexual favours from Cara tonight,' he said.

Or ever, he thought as he stuffed the doctor's card into his back pocket, the sting of guilt unmistakable.

Having Cara in his arms earlier, as he'd carried her into the suite, had caused a string of conflicting, confusing and contradictory emotions but even he could not deny the relentless surge of desire.

How could he have become aroused so easily? When she had been so fragile. Exhausted by a pregnancy which he had failed to prevent. Perhaps he wasn't that unlike his father after all. The thought sickened him, bringing back memories of his mother, and giving him an even more compelling reason to insist on marriage. He would not abandon the mother of his child while her health was at risk, the way his father had abandoned his mother.

'Mr Durand, please don't misconstrue what I said.' To his surprise, the doctor paused at the door, her face a picture of empathy. And understanding. 'I didn't intend to imply sexual intercourse between you is dangerous. It's not. As long as you're both willing, many couples continue sexual relations well into the third trimester. And, as I said, Ms Evans is healthy. She just needs a good rest. I think it would be wise, though, for you to bring her into the Harley Street clinic tomorrow so we can do an ultrasound.'

'You feel this is necessary?' Maxim asked, unable to hide his anxiety.

'Not necessary, but desirable,' the doctor said, touching his arm. 'To put both your minds at rest. It's not unusual for men to experience a loss of libido when their partner becomes pregnant. But I can assure you the changes to Cara's body are all perfectly natural.'

'Okay,' he said, feeling like a fraud. The doctor had misunderstood. A loss of libido was not the problem. 'I will bring Cara to the clinic tomorrow,' he added reluctantly.

He didn't want to think too much about the child just yet. Only Cara. But ensuring all was completely safe with the pregnancy made sense. Especially given the answering desire he'd seen in her eyes today.

She would be living in his home, with his ring on her finger, for four long months until the child was born if he got his way, which he would. The chances of them both being able to keep their hands off each other for that length of time were minimal, at best.

He could not let Cara out of his sight again,

until he had her promise that she would let him do what was best for her.

And that meant getting her to agree to marry him.

CHAPTER TEN

CARA'S EYELIDS FLUTTERED open and she found herself in an enormous room. The gold drapes of the four-poster bed in which she'd slept were illuminated by a strip of sunlight shining through the gap in the curtains drawn across a large picture window opposite the bed.

Was she dreaming? she wondered as her eyes adjusted to the half-light.

This was not the cramped, chilly room in the house she shared in Leyton, where the traffic noise from outside rattled the windows and woke her up at dawn each morning. Her limbs felt light, her mind refreshed, despite the familiar ache in her toes from the high heels she wore for work. When was the last time she'd woken up feeling this well rested?

She sat up and the sheet dropped into her lap, making her aware she was wearing nothing but her bra and panties. Where were her fluffy PJs?

The ripple of sensation became a flood as the

sleep cleared from her brain, and the events of the previous evening rushed in to fill the gap.

Maxim. Maxim had found her last night and brought her here.

The memories assailed her. His dark eyes—shocked, aroused, accusing. His voice—rough with tightly leashed outrage, then deep with reproach. The scent of him—sandalwood soap and man—invading her senses as she sat in the cab on the ride to his hotel, struggling to stay awake and focused. The strength of his arms—powerful, unyielding, supportive—as he scooped her up when her knees turned to water in the lift. His hands—gentle yet brusque in the shadows of the ornate room as he undressed her and tucked the quilt around her after the doctor's visit, and she lost her battle with exhaustion.

She shivered, even though the room was the perfect ambient temperature, and the familiar heat at the memory of his touch glowed in her belly.

This is my flesh and blood. Do you really believe I would choose to abandon it?

What had she done? She had assumed he would be furious if he ever found out about the child, and her decision to have it, but all she could remember from his expression was the flash of hurt.

I am not my father.

The heat in her stomach became sharp and jagged.

She'd judged him and condemned him. And while her decision to run away had been sound, he was right: everything had changed once she had discovered her pregnancy. She placed her palm on the firm bulge of her stomach, felt the flutter of movement which had scared her a week ago but now reassured her.

'Good morning, pipsqueak,' she murmured, as she did every morning. She let a tear trail down her cheek—because there was no one to see it. 'I'm so sorry,' she whispered, swiping the tear away with the back of her hand.

Running had become a default after she'd left care, because it had always been easier to start afresh than to face her fears. She should have realised as soon as the doctor had told her she was expecting Maxim Durand's child that now was the time to stop running, but it was pointless beating herself up about that panicked decision now.

He'd found her, and last night, despite his shock, he had seemed much more furious about the fact she hadn't told him about the baby...*his* baby...than he was about the pregnancy itself.

The choice would always have been yours.

She'd made a mistake not contacting Maxim. Maybe she'd made it for the right reasons. He was still rich and ruthless and as overwhelming as he'd always been. But recognising her mistake now was the only way to move forward.

She slipped out of the bed. Her bare feet sunk into the thick luxurious carpet as she padded over to an armchair upholstered in embroidered silk, where someone had draped a thick bathrobe.

She shrugged it on, and then opened the curtains on the room's huge picture window to find a balcony overlooking a striking view of the River Thames.

She shoved her hands into the pockets of the robe, then glanced back at the bed. The pillow next to hers lay untouched. He hadn't joined her during the night.

She recalled his touch the evening before. Not urgent and intense, but gentle and impersonal. The weight in her stomach twisted and plunged.

For goodness' sake, Cara, what did you expect? Of course he isn't interested in you any more. And why would you want him to be? You're a pregnant woman, and it was your inability to resist him that got you into this fix in the first place.

She pressed her fists towards her belly, sending a silent apology to the life growing inside her.

You're not a problem, pipsqueak. Or a fix. And you never will be, okay?

Although pretty much everything else in her life was, she thought ruefully.

She'd lost her job last night. Martha would never rehire her after she'd run out on her shift like a madwoman. And somehow or other she was going to have to set aside her guilt at not contacting Maxim a lot sooner and find a solution which would suit them both—without letting him steamroller her.

She drew in a breath, overwhelmed at the thought of navigating that conversation.

Maxim, being Maxim, had been forceful and demanding last night, riding roughshod over her protests and basically taking matters into his own hands—or, rather, arms. She'd been way too exhausted to object. But this morning she was going to need to start standing up for herself.

She brushed her hair back from her face. It was still early, she realised, analysing the angle of the sun over the Thames. The first order of business was to have a shower and find her clothes, then she'd be ready to face him. And ready to face the mistake she'd made not contacting him.

But she wasn't the only one to blame for what had happened, she told herself staunchly.

She wasn't the one who had chosen to use their night together in a cynical bid to acquire a property—the one who had been so hell-bent on revenge he had decided to throw her to the media wolves.

Maxim was not blameless in this calamity.

Once she was washed and dressed, she'd be ready to point that out to him—a bit more forcefully than she had last night.

Twenty minutes later, Cara was clean and dry, her damp hair brushed. Unfortunately, she still only had the bathrobe and yesterday's underwear to wear because she'd been unable to find her clothes. Or her shoes. Even her coat had disappeared.

Had Maxim stolen them? Or hidden them? To keep her docile and trapped in this room?

Bolstering her newfound courage, she tightened the tie on the robe and eased open the bedroom door.

Expecting him to be waiting for her in the sitting room, she let go of the breath she'd been holding as she scanned the suite's large, luxuriously decorated lounge area and couldn't see him anywhere.

But then a gruff sound had her gaze zeroing in on the back of the three-seater sofa facing another large picture window, which was the feature aspect of the lavish room. A pair of bare feet, long and tanned, hung over the cream silk arm of the sofa.

Maxim?

Her throat tightened as she walked round the sofa to find his tall frame stretched out on the cushions, taking up all the available space. A thin blanket covered the lower half of his body, the waistband of his boxer shorts peeking out. Her heartbeat throbbed in her throat and the weight in her stomach plunged as her greedy gaze studied him unobserved. His bare chest looked as magnificent as she remembered it, while his flat stomach rose and fell in a steady rhythm which echoed in her abdomen. There was a tuft of dark hair under one arm where he'd lifted it over his head, probably in a vain attempt to get comfortable. His usually swept-back wavy hair was ruffled, and mushed on one side, while the shadow of beard scruff covered his jaw.

She assumed most men looked less intimidating while they were asleep.

Not Maxim.

If anything, the sight of him, his body relaxed and yet no less powerful, his nakedness making him all the more compelling, was having the opposite effect.

Her breath shuddered out.

The quiet huff had his eyes snapping open. Instantly alert, his golden gaze narrowed. And she found herself taking a step back.

'*Bonjour*, Cara,' he said, clearly having no problem remembering exactly what had happened the previous evening.

He yawned and stretched then sat up, his movements indolent and yet focused.

Why did she suddenly feel as if she'd ventured into the wolf's den? Again.

Every one of her pulse points throbbed, the edgy tension in her body intensifying as he threw off the blanket to reveal hard thighs and long legs, furred with hair. She could also see the prominent length pressing against the front of his boxers.

The weight in her stomach became hot and achy, beating a chaotic pulse in her sex.

He thrust his fingers through his hair, sweeping the silky waves back, scrubbed his hands down his face—then sent her a humourless smile.

'Ignore it. I get one every morning. Especially if I have been dreaming of you.'

The blush climbed into her cheeks, making her feel painfully gauche. And stupidly light-headed.

What on earth was that about? She didn't want him to dream about her… Did she?

'Where are my clothes, Maxim?' she blurted out, unsettled, not just by the intimacy of the moment but also her ludicrous reaction to it.

She needed to leave. They could talk about everything later, when she'd regained her equilibrium. When she wasn't standing in his hotel suite too aware of her nakedness under the robe… And his prominent morning erection.

Instead of replying, though, he stood and

arched his back, then tilted his head to one side then the other. She heard the joints popping in his neck, making the tightness in her throat increase—at the thought that he had slept all night on the couch in his own luxury suite so she could get her first good night's sleep in weeks.

'I had them destroyed,' he said, the husky tone completely unapologetic.

The statement had all her warm feelings evaporating.

'You...*what*?' She wanted to be outraged at his arrogance, but all she felt was more exposed. And wary. 'Why?'

'To prevent you from running away while I was asleep,' he said without even a hint of remorse.

'But... You... That's... You had no right,' she sputtered, finally managing to grab hold of some outrage. She'd had to pay for that uniform out of her own money.

'I had every right,' he said as his gaze strayed down to her midriff. 'I don't intend to let you vanish again until we have a few things settled.'

'But I wasn't going to vanish,' she said, stunned by the inflexible tone. And the arrogance behind it. And wondering what things he intended to settle. 'I told you last night I'd come back here to talk to you today.'

He didn't even give her the benefit of an answer this time, simply lifted one sceptical brow, his expression saying in all but words: *Do I look like an idiot?*

She wanted to shout and rail against his lack of trust. But she was forced to concede he had a point, given her previous disappearing act. 'Those clothes were my property. I paid for them and I need them because I'm going to have to find another job today. So thanks a bunch for that,' she said, trying to hide her distress behind a wall of sarcasm.

Showing weakness to Maxim Durand was not a good idea. She'd shown him weakness last night in her exhaustion and he'd steamrollered over all her protests, not to mention destroying her property.

The cynical expression disappeared but, just when she thought she'd finally scored a point, he said in a voice so calm and forceful and pragmatic it took a moment for her to register the outrageousness of what he had said, 'You do not need those clothes, as I will buy you better ones. And you don't need a job, because we are to be married in France as soon as it is possible, in ten days' time.'

'Are you...? Are you crazy?'

Maxim watched the light flush on Cara's

cheeks deepen to magenta—and the wary concern in her bright blue gaze turn to panic.

Okay, perhaps that had not been the best way to propose. She'd retreated another step, as if trying to edge away from a dangerous animal which was about to pounce.

She was right to be cautious. His emotions had never been this volatile before, this uncontrolled. As soon as he'd opened his eyes, and seen her standing by his makeshift bed, her hair damp and her curves swamped in the fluffy bathrobe, he'd had to quell the primal urge to leap forward and claim her, scared she would disappear again, as she had so many times before in his dreams, and nightmares.

In fact, for one split second he'd thought she might be an apparition, caused by the loss of blood from his head fuelling the painful erection which had woken him every morning for five long months.

'Let me explain, Cara,' he said, taking a step forward. 'Marriage is the obvious solution.'

She scuttled back another step. 'Don't… Don't touch me, Maxim. I mean it.' She held her hands up in the universal sign of surrender, her gaze darting across the suite to the door. 'I have to leave. I can't…'

She made a dash round the sofa. Without thinking, he leapt over the obstacle and captured her wrist, drawing her to a halt.

She struggled, trying to tug her hand free. 'Let me go, Maxim… I want to leave.'

'Stop, Cara. You will hurt yourself,' he said, drawing her against his body, quelling her struggles in his embrace as he pressed her gently against the wall, caging her in.

He inhaled her scent, wild flowers and woman, the scent that had driven him mad last night as he undressed her—and forced himself not to touch her more than was absolutely necessary.

At last she stilled and he heard the stifled sob as her forehead pressed against his sternum.

He felt like a brute, a beast. The jagged sound of her breathing—the painful attempt to hold onto her tears, and the hopelessness that he suspected lay behind it—cut into his composure, his equilibrium. His heart expanded in his chest and his throat closed. But he couldn't let her go, not like this. Not now he had found her. If he let her run, he might never find her again, and he wouldn't be able to live with himself—knowing she was out there somewhere, surviving on nothing, endangering herself, when he had the means to protect her. He had failed his mother once. He would not fail her.

'Shh, Cara,' he murmured against her hair.

She shuddered, the sounds of her breathing cutting off as she tried to hold onto her emotions.

'I would never hurt you,' he said, as softly as he could. 'You have my word. But I cannot let you leave until you have agreed to marry me.'

She sniffed, the sound enough to unlock the strangling feeling in his throat.

How had they come to this? And how could they repair the damage between them? He had planted a child inside her. A child which had sapped all of her strength. Given her virgin state five months ago, he had to take full responsibility for that.

He brushed the damp hair back from her cheek, then cradled her face to lift her gaze to his. Her cheeks were dry but he could see the moisture in the deep pools of shattered blue.

Heat surged in his groin. He steeled himself against it. Now was the time to soothe rather than demand—not a skill he was particularly adept at. He must not ignite the passion between them, even if he could smell the musky scent of her arousal. And see the stunned desire in her eyes.

She did not understand the depth and power of their physical connection because she had so little experience. But he did.

He placed a light kiss on her forehead, felt her shudder of response and then forced himself to drop his arms and release her from the protective cage.

She stood watching him. Unsure, shaky, but he took it as a major concession that, rather than try to run, she simply wrapped her arms around her waist, as if attempting to hold onto the emotions cascading through her body.

Emotions he recognised because they were cascading through his body too. Emotions she probably didn't understand any more than he did.

'The marriage would be time-limited,' he said, his voice rough as he struggled to get his mind to engage with the plans he'd made last night. Detailed, pragmatic, sensible plans before he'd managed to shoot them to hell with his knee-jerk demands.

Her eyes widened and her expression was still stunned, still confused, still a little panicked. But she didn't speak and she didn't move, so he forced himself to continue in a voice he hoped was more persuasive than demanding. Another new experience for him.

'I want the child to be born with my name— and to always have my protection.'

And I want you to have my name and my protection too.

He swallowed, forcing himself not to add the qualifier, the truth of which surged through him as she stood before him, virtually naked, and utterly defenceless.

'I want you to live in Burgundy at my *château*, to have the best possible *prénatal* care. No more working, no more hunger, no more exhaustion. I will...' He paused, forced himself to counter the desire to demand. 'I *wish* to provide for you everything you need while you bear this child. This is very important to me.'

She watched him but, instead of refusing his help out of hand as he half expected her to do—for she was nothing if not contrary, and fiercely independent—she simply said softly, 'Why?'

'Why do I wish this?' he asked, confused. *Was this not obvious?* 'Because I do not wish for you to put your life at risk...' He breathed, paused, before blurting out too much. 'Simply to survive, when I have the money you need.'

'My life's not at risk, Maxim.' Her gaze softened, drawing him in, while only frustrating him more. 'Why would you think that?'

His brow knotted. Was this a trick question? But she didn't look conniving, she looked guileless and unsure, so he was forced to answer the question. To spell out the obvious.

'Pregnancy and childbirth *is* dangerous, Cara. Women can be...' He breathed, the memories burning like acid on his tongue. 'Women can be weakened by childbirth, especially without the appropriate care. We shouldn't have had sex without a condom.' He allowed his gaze to stray to the pronounced bulge of her belly, the guilt he had tried to qualify and mitigate during the night starting to overwhelm him. 'It is through my carelessness that you are now facing this danger. So it is my duty to ensure you are well cared for until the child is born.'

He lifted his gaze to hers, ready to demand, beg, cajole, even blackmail her if necessary into agreeing to the marriage. But he stopped, shocked by the sheen of tears in Cara's eyes. 'What is wrong?'

The stab of guilt lanced into his belly. He hadn't meant to distress her more. Had only wanted to give her the explanation she sought— so she would see why marriage was the only answer.

'Maxim, I'm really not in any danger,' Cara said. 'And, even if I were, you're not responsible.'

'Of course I am,' he said, his voice prickly with impatience. But for once she welcomed the caustic reaction because it revealed so much.

Going with instinct, she pressed a hand to the rough stubble on his jaw.

A muscle in his cheek tensed before he drew back, his expression confused and wary, but also more vulnerable than she had ever seen him. Or ever suspected he could be.

'How can you pretend this is not my fault?' he said.

'Because I made a conscious choice to have this child,' she said, trying to pick her way through the minefield he had exposed. She had underestimated him in so many ways, she realised. That he should feel such responsibility for her health and well-being was ridiculous, but she had helped exacerbate it because of her own stubborn pride, her refusal to bend.

She should have contacted him as soon as she'd found out about her condition. If she had asked for his support she would not have had to work herself into exhaustion. And scared him to this degree.

'I could have ended this pregnancy but I didn't want to,' she said. 'You're not responsible for the choice I made to have this child.'

She'd been a coward, scared he would object to her keeping the baby. And, because of her fear, she hadn't given him a choice.

'This is a pointless argument, Cara.' His gaze slipped to her stomach again, and she could see the anxiety about her condition flicker across his face before his gaze met hers.

· What was it about the pregnancy that disturbed him so much?

'The fact is you are pregnant, you are having this child.' She saw his Adam's apple bob as he swallowed and realised how hard it was for him to say the next word. '*My* child. I do not want you to be harmed.'

Her heart swelled painfully in her chest. 'I won't be harmed, Maxim,' she said, struggling not to make too much of his determination to care for her, when no other man ever had. 'I'm pregnant, not sick.'

'Pregnancy is dangerous. My own mother...'

He stopped, his eyes becoming shuttered, the naked emotions she'd seen flash across his face ruthlessly controlled. But it was already too late. She'd seen the agony when he'd mentioned his mother.

'What happened to your mother, Maxim?'

He shifted back, withdrawing even further. 'It is of no importance,' he said.

But she could see it was of considerable importance. Was this why he was so determined to marry her, to provide for her? Was his mother the reason why he was so concerned about the pregnancy?

'Did she... Did she have a difficult pregnancy?' she asked softly. 'Is that why mine scares you?' she probed gently, covering her bump with her hand.

He thrust his fingers through his hair. But she'd

seen the shocking answer to her question, the shudder of remembered trauma in his eyes before he could mask it. 'I was a big baby,' he said. 'She was a small woman. And he refused to pay for the care she needed.' He looked away, his voice brittle with anguish. 'And I was not the only child he failed to prevent. She had two miscarriages before he finally discarded her.'

'Maxim, I'm so sorry,' Cara whispered, touching his arm, feeling the muscles tense. Had he witnessed these miscarriages? He must have, the shadow of trauma in his eyes was unmistakable. 'I wish I'd known him for what he really was,' she said forcefully, realising how foolish she had been to ever stand up for her old employer. 'I never would have agreed to marry him.' How could she have been so blind to Pierre de la Mare's faults?

'You are not to blame,' he said, and she could see he didn't blame her. 'My father spent a lifetime manipulating women. He was very good at it.' He blinked, the flush of colour on his cheeks making her realise how hard it was for him to talk about his parents' relationship. 'My mother never stopped loving him, despite the way he treated her.' He huffed out an unsteady breath, the confusion in his eyes so poignant she felt her heart butt her tonsils. 'But none of that is important now. What *is* important is that you do not suffer, the way she did. I cannot let that happen, or I will be no better than him.'

She nodded, tears welling in her eyes—he'd said yesterday that he wasn't his father; she hadn't realised how much he'd meant by that. 'I… I understand.'

'I would not have chosen to become a father, Cara,' he said, gruff pain in his voice, devoid of accusation but so full of regret it made her heart hurt. 'But I did not take the precautions I could have to ensure this did not happen, and now you must face the consequences of my actions.' He made the baby sound like a terrible burden. And obviously to him it was, she thought miserably. 'I also know what it is not to have a father's protection, a father's name and wealth. So I cannot allow my own child to grow up without these things.'

Cara nodded again.

But a good father could provide so much more than that. When her own mother had died, she'd looked to her father to provide not just financial but also emotional security. And he'd failed. He'd discarded her and rejected her—because she was too much trouble and he had never really loved her. The same way Pierre de la Mare had discarded and rejected Maxim.

'Would you…? Would you be able to offer this

baby more than that, Maxim?' she asked, scared to hope, but more scared not to ask.

'What do you mean?' he said, looking genuinely perplexed by the question, and her heart stumbled in her chest.

'Do you think you could offer the child more than just your name and your protection?'

He frowned, as if he hadn't expected the question. 'I doubt that is a possibility. As I said, I never planned to become a father, Cara, precisely because I do not think I would be good at it.'

The words were said gently, firmly, but even so the spurt of hope refused to die. He hadn't categorically ruled the possibility out.

Both their fathers had been incapable of love. But she refused to believe it had to be like that. She already loved their child so much. And while the kind of marriage Maxim was talking about— a time-limited marriage, simply for the purposes of protecting her and giving his child his name— wasn't enough, the fact that he was so desperate to offer her and their child security was a start.

Maxim had been rejected the same way she had. She knew exactly how much that hurt. How it could make you doubt yourself, make you lose confidence in your ability to love. She'd discovered in the last five months—from the first moment when the blue line had appeared on the test kit to that flutter of movement a week ago—a vast well of love she'd never realised she was capable of.

The baby wasn't real to Maxim, the way it was to her.

But from their interaction that first night, when he had tended her and the next morning, when he had tried to persuade her to become his mistress, she knew he wasn't an insensitive man. Even blinded by his need for revenge against Pierre, he'd tried to do the right thing by her.

She also knew that he'd witnessed enough of his parents' relationship to be deeply cynical about love. But surely that didn't mean he couldn't one day be a good father.

'Is that why you were so determined to destroy La Maison?' she asked, as what he had said about his mother and the trauma of the miscarriages he must have witnessed shed new light on his actions that night, and the morning after. 'Is that why you exposed me to the press? Because of what happened to your mother—and you—in that house?' she finished softly. The memory of how he had betrayed her still hurt, but maybe that betrayal had never been about her, maybe it had always been about his past—a way to avenge his mother as well as himself, against the man who had used his mother so callously, and then discarded them both.

'What? No.' He swore softly, looking shocked.

'It was just an error. Some intern at the *advocat*'s office forgot to delete the attached affidavit before sending out a press statement that I was challenging the will. Believe me when I say I would never have revealed details of our sex life to the press deliberately. And I am not so insane as to blame my mother's suffering on a house.'

She smiled at his indignation, as the tightness in her chest, which had been there ever since that morning, dissolved. 'That's good to know.'

His gaze intensified, searing her skin all over again.

'Surely you can see we must be wed now, Cara?'

The roughened 'R' as he said her name seemed to stroke across her swollen clitoris, making her powerless to deny the yearning this time. The silence in the room seemed to vibrate around them both, making her more aware of the liquid pull which had been there ever since she had first set eyes on him.

'*épouse-moi, Cara*,' he murmured in guttural French.

Marry me, Cara.

He closed the gap between them and kissed her neck, sensing her weakness and exploiting it.

She arched against him as a sob of desire burst out of her mouth.

Need arrowed down, making her tender breasts

ache and swell, and the sweet spot between her thighs engorge in a rush as he suckled the pulse point under her earlobe.

His breathing became as ragged as hers but, before she could surrender to the sensations surging through her body and give him the answer he wanted, she felt the familiar flutter of movement in her womb.

Maxim jerked back, his brows launching up his forehead.

'*C'est le bébé?*' he asked.

She nodded, unable to contain her grin—or the choking sensation in her throat—at his horrified expression. 'Yes, it likes to kick.'

Going with instinct, she untied her bathrobe, took his limp hand, placed it on her naked belly, then pressed down. The baby responded instantly, not that impressed with having its living space impeded.

His dark gaze was stunned and wary when it met hers. '*Il est très fort, ce bébé,*' he murmured. 'It does not hurt you?'

'No,' she said, unable to resist a sad smile at his question, knowing it came from a place of fear. 'The obstetrician last night said it's just extremely active… Most women don't feel the baby's kick until twenty-five weeks in a first pregnancy. But it's perfectly natural and just a sign of how healthy the baby is.'

She knew she was babbling but he didn't seem to notice as he stared at her stomach as if he were trying to see right through the skin to his child beneath.

His hand slipped away from her stomach, before he nodded. 'Dr Karim suggested we go to her clinic this morning for an ultrasound,' he said. He glanced at his watch. 'The concierge can bring some new clothes to the suite this morning to replace the ones that were destroyed. Once you are dressed, we can leave for Harley Street.'

It wasn't a question, it was a demand, his gaze fixed on her face with its usual intensity, daring her to refuse him.

She sighed. Even though Dr Karim had been wonderful last night, she didn't need an expensive Harley Street doctor when she already had a great obstetrics team at her local NHS hospital. But now she knew why it was so important to him to give her the best medical care money could buy, she didn't have the heart to refuse him.

'All right, Maxim. If you insist,' she said.

'I do,' he said, as she knew he would.

'I guess I should be grateful you're going to supply me with clothes first,' she managed, trying to lighten the mood before the emotion in her throat strangled her. Perhaps she was being naïve and too hopeful. But it felt like a positive step to have him care about the baby's welfare, even if it did come from an irrational fear.

'I am being very magnanimous,' he murmured as he braced his hands above her head, caging her in again. 'As I much prefer you naked.'

She laughed, but the sound came out husky and strained, the heat in her core flaring again. Surely his willingness to flirt with her again was also a good sign, she thought a little desperately.

Pressing his forehead to hers, Maxim murmured, 'Cara, you must marry me. Please say yes.'

Unlike before, the proposal wasn't a demand. Instead, he sounded tense, wary, concerned. Her stomach dropped, the faint flutters of the baby's kicks almost as if their child was giving its assent.

He lifted his head, his expression strained but conciliatory. 'I want you to be safe. Can you not see it is madness for you to work when there is no need? I have money. Let me spend it on you both, at least until the child is born.'

The emotion that had been so carefully contained welled up her chest. She dropped her gaze. 'I don't… I don't feel comfortable having you support me,' she managed round the huge boulder that was starting to choke her.

She understood why he needed to do this. He wasn't trying to take her independence away from her. She understood that now too. This was about protecting her, the way his mother had not been protected by his father.

But it was still hard for her to contemplate putting her life into his hands, however temporarily—it had been so long since she'd been able to trust anyone with her well-being. She'd always relied on herself. And, okay, maybe she had taken some foolish risks, working long hours for minimal pay. But she wasn't fragile.

He tucked a knuckle under her chin and lifted her gaze. 'There is no shame in needing support,' he said.

Her lips quirked. Did he realise how ironic that sounded coming from him, a man she suspected had made a point of never needing anyone's support?

'What is funny about this?' He frowned, the prickly frustration back. But this time she could see his temper was simply a mask for his deeper feelings—feelings that compelled him to do whatever it took to be a better man than his father.

She shook her head. 'Nothing, really,' she said, her thoughts sobering. 'Why couldn't I just come to live in Burgundy until the baby is born? We really don't need to be married.'

'Yes, we do,' he said in that dictatorial tone she had come to recognise. But somehow, this time, she could hear the emotion behind the command. 'I do not want my child born without a father,' he added. 'If you will agree to marry me, we can work out an arrangement that will satisfy us both. I would need you to sign a prenuptial agreement, so that we can dissolve the marriage as soon as the baby is born with the minimum of fuss.'

She tried not to let the thought sadden her that this marriage—if she agreed to it—would already have a sell-by date. Surely that would be in her best interests, as well as his? Ultimately the marriage wasn't important in itself, what mattered was that while she was living in his home, and preparing to bear his child, he would have the chance to come to terms with the reality of his role in its life. And perhaps overcome his objections to being its father in more than just name only.

'What about… What about custody?' she asked.

'A child must stay with its mother,' he said without hesitation, which had the bubble of desperate hope twisting in her chest. Did he have any intention of seeing the child after its birth?

Don't despair, Cara, he's only known about his child for one day—you've known about it for months.

'But I would ask that you allow me to support the child once the marriage is over,' he added.

Emotion welled in her throat, at the simple and unequivocal statement.

'Of course,' she said, determined to give him

the time he needed. The truth was she wanted so much more from him for this child than just financial security. She wanted him to forge an emotional connection to it.

At the moment, that was not what he was offering. But surely that could change, if she could break down some of the barriers he had put around his heart? And overcome his fear of fatherhood, which was the hideous legacy of his own childhood. This marriage would give her four precious months to do that…

'So will you marry me, and come to Burgundy until the child is born?' The curt demand had a sobering effect.

Was she seriously considering saying yes?

This was a business arrangement for Maxim in many ways. A way for him to discharge his responsibilities to his child, make amends for the wrongs done to his mother and ensure that he was better than his father. And she was fairly certain her reasons for wanting to spend more time with Maxim weren't nearly as pragmatic.

But surely the chance of giving her child something she had never had—a father, in every sense of the word—was worth the risk?

'Okay, Maxim,' she murmured, determined to focus on the hope and not the fear.

She didn't want to be a coward any more. She'd taken so many crucial decisions away from

Maxim with her silence, decisions she couldn't and wouldn't change, but this was a decision they could make together. And maybe, just maybe, it could lead to more.

'I'll marry you,' she said.

CHAPTER ELEVEN

'Do you want to know the sex of the child?'

Maxim blinked, barely able to register Dr Karim's question, still stunned by the image on the screen, and the loud, rapid tick coming from the ultrasound equipment, which the obstetrician had informed them was the heartbeat.

It had a head, a face, tiny fingers and toes already forming, its long legs folded up and practically touching its nose. No wonder it kicked so much, it looked cramped in there.

His child. His baby. Not abstract now, but tangible, and real... And so terrifying he was struggling to breathe.

'Can you tell?' Cara asked the doctor, breathless and excited. 'At my last scan they didn't know.'

'We just got a very good shot of the genitals,' the doctor said. 'So I can say with some degree of certainty. But it's really up to you if you want to know, or would rather wait.'

'Maxim? What do you think?' Cara asked him, her face flushed with pleasure.

He didn't have an answer for her. He didn't know if he could stand to have this moment be any more real than it already was. He was starting to sweat, the blue walls of the luxury suite closing in around him and the memories of that day so long ago playing through his head on a loop.

'Ne me quitte pas, Maxim. J'ai besoin de toi.'
Don't leave me, Maxim. I need you.

How could he possibly protect this tiny vulnerable creature from harm? When he had failed to protect his own mother?

'I don't...' He coughed to ease the tightness in his throat, and banish the vicious memories. 'I don't have a preference. You can decide,' he managed. Did it really matter what sex this child was, when he could never be a part of its life?

The sparkle of excitement in Cara's eyes dimmed. He steeled himself against the vicious stab of guilt. He had already told her what he could offer, and what he could not. The child would have his name, his wealth and his protection, always, and that would have to be enough. He had nothing more to offer.

'I'd like to know then,' Cara murmured, turning back to the doctor.

Dr Karim smiled and pointed out something on the monitor with a wand. 'Obviously, I can't be one hundred per cent certain, but I'm fairly sure what we have here is a penis,' she said with a chuckle.

'A boy?' Cara said, her tone thick with a hushed reverence that only made the hollow weight in Maxim's stomach plunge. She turned and gripped his fingers. 'Did you hear that, Maxim—we're having a son.'

He nodded, then lifted her fingers to his lips, barely able to speak round the shame threatening to choke him. 'I should go,' he said. 'To make the rest of the arrangements.'

'Arrangements?' she said, looking confused.

'I must return to France today. I have arranged for you to remain at the hotel in London until the marriage can be performed at the *mairie* in Auxerre in ten days' time.'

Why had he agreed to come to this appointment? It had been a foolish impulse that he now regretted. He'd never expected the child to be recognisable this early in its gestation. 'I will see you at the airport in Burgundy. Remember to rest.'

'I won't see you for ten days?' she asked.

He steeled himself against the tightness in his chest caused by the stunned dismay in her eyes. 'Yes, I am afraid it takes ten days to do the documentation before we can be married.'

Something he was pathetically grateful for.

He had planned to suggest they marry in London, but he was far too aware, even now, of Cara's lush figure beneath the clinic's starched robe. He still wanted her too much, even knowing that a life grew inside her. He needed this ten-day separation to ensure he got his hunger for her under some semblance of control.

'You must rest,' he said to Cara. 'Doctor, thank you,' he murmured, turning to the obstetrician.

Saying his goodbyes, he placed a kiss on Cara's forehead, then made his escape from the airless room. Leaving the fear, and the memories and the insistent hunger behind him. For the time being at least. The weight in his stomach expanded.

He had ten days to pull himself together and seal off the raw, aching hole that had opened up in the pit of his stomach on seeing the image of his child.

His son.

And ten days to figure out how he was going to survive four endless months of marriage without jumping his son's mother every single chance he got.

CHAPTER TWELVE

THE CAVALCADE OF black SUVs crested the hill. Cara's breath caught as Maxim's home appeared in the distance. Château Durand's centuries-old stone architecture dominated the surrounding fields, making a defiant statement about the power and wealth of the man she had just married in a short civil ceremony at Auxerre town hall.

She'd never ventured onto Durand Corporation land during her months in Burgundy as the de la Mare housekeeper, but she'd heard all the local whispers about the derelict *château* Maxim Durand had bought and then spent a fortune renovating in the last few years.

Nothing could have prepared her, though, for the magnificence of the property as they drove towards it from the heliport at the winery complex where they'd touched down twenty minutes ago.

They drove through the gates in the high stone wall, making their way past a series of brick outbuildings before travelling along the driveway that led through lavish, perfectly manicured gardens designed in a geometric pattern Capability Brown would have been proud of. The house itself—not a house, a mansion—loomed large at the end of the drive, three storeys of elegant arched windows with pale green shutters. Wisteria and ivy clung to the stonework to add a fanciful charm, while the intricate wrought iron balconies on the upper levels and the red tiled roof blended perfectly with the turrets on each end of the imposing building, giving it the appearance of a castle fit for a king.

Cara risked a glance at her husband, who was busy speaking to someone in rapid French on his mobile phone. Maxim might not have been born a king, but he suited the role perfectly.

Had it really been ten days ago that she had agreed to marry him? The last week and a half had gone by in a blur. The days had merged into one, each one dominated by some new task: the meetings with Maxim's legal team to outline the prenup he was offering her, which seemed scrupulously fair; the appointments with a barrage of stylists; the fittings with the couturier who had designed and made a whole new wardrobe for her in record time, not to mention the chauffeur-driven trip to say goodbye to Dora, who had been starry-eyed at the mention of who Cara was marrying.

But during the nights Cara had missed Maxim, feeling alone and confused in the hotel's luxury suite.

Her fevered mind had had far too much time, going over every moment of their relationship so far, and especially the last time she'd seen him, in Dr Karim's surgery in Harley Street—and the stricken look on his face when their baby…she breathed…their *son* had appeared on the monitor.

There had been no sign of that haunted look this morning when he'd met her at the airport. Perhaps she had imagined it?

There had certainly been no time to question him before they'd been whisked to the *mairie* to say their vows, before heading to a heliport for the breathtaking ride to the Durand estate.

She pulled the brand-new smartphone she'd been given by one of Maxim's army of assistants out of the pocket of the new linen trousers she wore—part of the beautiful new trousseau that had arrived yesterday. Maxim had arranged to have her belongings brought from her room in Leyton, but her battered rucksack now sat in the back of this pristine SUV, among a pile of matching hand-tooled luggage with her initials stamped on them.

Her *new* initials. CED. Cara Evans Durand.

She checked the time, trying to ground herself, and get rid of the tightness that had gripped her chest ever since she'd stepped out of his private jet, to see him waiting for her on the tarmac.

Two o'clock in the afternoon. She huffed out an unsteady breath and stared through the car's window as the line of vehicles entered a leafy courtyard at the side of Maxim's palace. She could see a large pool shaded by trees, covered now for the winter months, at the far end of a manicured lawn which led down from the *château*'s back terrace.

Of course he had a pool! She'd never even visited somewhere this lavish, let alone lived in such a place.

She'd known Maxim was wealthy. But she'd had no idea of the extent of his wealth, and power, and how he wielded that power so effortlessly, until the last ten days. His home was simply the crowning glory.

The car stopped and Maxim ended his latest call. After stepping out of the car, he skirted the bonnet, spoke to one of his assistants then arrived to grasp the door handle before she could open the door for herself.

'Welcome to Château Durand, Cara,' he said, sending her a distracted smile. He clicked his fingers and two footmen rushed out of the long line of uniformed staff waiting at the *château*'s door to greet them.

'Your new French obstetrician and her team are waiting to check you over,' Maxim said as the footmen began collecting her luggage from the boot. His large hand settled on the small of her back, to direct her up the marble stairs to the *château*'s entrance. Shivers rippled up her spine where his fingers touched.

'But I had another check-up with Dr Karim yesterday,' she said.

'It is only a formality,' he murmured, rubbing her back as he guided her, making the shivers increase. 'Once the doctor is happy,' he said, 'it is probably best if you take a rest in your rooms before tonight.'

Her *rooms*? Why did she need more than one? And what was happening tonight? Was he talking about consummating their marriage?

He glanced at his watch. 'Does six o'clock suit you?'

'You're scheduling sex?' Her shocked question burst out before she could think better or it. After all, she'd had far too much time to think about this aspect of their relationship in the last ten days, while lying alone in her hotel bed.

His lips quirked in a wry smile, but his intense gaze had a blush firing into her cheeks.

'I was talking of the wedding, Cara,' he said, the arousal in his eyes unmistakable at the mention of sex.

'Oh, I… I see.' She'd never felt more gauche

or stupid—or needy—in her life. 'But aren't we already married?' she murmured.

She'd assumed the quick ceremony at the town hall in Auxerre was all they needed to do. Had actually been grateful for the secular, perfunctory nature of the proceedings. It was going to be hard enough to keep the reality of their marriage clear in her mind while living in Maxim's lavish home for the next few months.

'Yes, but we need a wedding ceremony, so that I can introduce you as my wife,' he said. 'There is a chapel in the grounds which has been prepared for the event, and my kitchen staff have arranged a wedding banquet in the *château*'s great hall.'

A *banquet*?

'But, I… *Really*?'

How had he arranged all this in little more than a week? And why?

She'd assumed there would be no ceremony. The less this felt like a real marriage the better. But Maxim seemed to have other ideas.

'Do not concern yourself,' he said. 'The stylist assured me she has provided a suitable dress in your trousseau.'

She had? Was it one of the numerous outfits she'd tried on? Why had no one told her it was a wedding dress?

He proceeded to introduce her to a few of his senior staff. Cara dutifully shook hands and spoke to them in her faltering French. The whole episode started to feel surreal as Maxim directed her into the house.

The *château* was as lavish inside as it was outside. Her breathing became ragged as Maxim led her past the downstairs salons and parlours and she glimpsed the bespoke antique furniture and a selection of stark modern pieces which looked equally expensive and intimidating. They walked up the wide sweeping staircase at the end of the entrance hall to the first floor, his hand on her back the only thing that was anchoring her now.

He left her at the door to a series of bright, airy, lavishly furnished rooms—*her rooms*, apparently—and introduced her to the obstetrician and two nurses he'd flown in from Paris.

'Wait, Maxim.' She stepped onto the landing to grasp the sleeve of his suit jacket. 'Will there be a lot of people at the wedding banquet?'

'Just some local dignitaries and my friends and colleagues,' he said. 'No more than a hundred in total.'

A hundred people? She actually felt sick.

He laughed, an indulgent sound that didn't do much for her panic attack, then cradled her cheek with his palm. 'Do not worry. It will be over sooner than you think.'

At which point...what? Were they going to

consummate this relationship? Not that she'd been obsessing over that question… Much.

Stop worrying about sex… attending a wedding banquet with a hundred people is quite intimidating enough.

'But I… I'm not… I have no experience of these sorts of social events,' she said as the fierce need continued to throb in her sex.

He placed his hand on her neck, stroked the rioting pulse point with his thumb and placed a kiss on her forehead. 'Do not panic, Cara, it will be okay. My assistant, Jean-Claude, has invited Marcel Caron to attend on your behalf, so there will be a familiar face. Marcel has offered to give you away, if you are happy with that arrangement?'

'I… I guess,' she said, surprised he had gone to the trouble of inviting Pierre's lawyer. 'But I really don't…'

'Shh…' He silenced her with another kiss. 'As my wife, you must get used to attending such events.'

She must? She'd had no idea he was going to expect her to behave like a real wife. She'd thought she was just supposed to be living here until the baby was born.

'But… I…?' She tried again to voice her fears, but he covered her mouth with his, silencing her again. The gentle kiss quickly became firm, seeking, persuasive, taking on a life of its own.

She answered his passion instinctively, desire rising to suffuse her whole body in undulating, unstoppable waves. She was panting, trembling with need, when he finally tore his mouth away.

'Do not fear, Cara. I will not leave your side once the ceremony starts,' he said, his gaze shuttered, and so intense it burned.

She stood shaking on the threshold of her rooms, watching him jog back down the stairs as the passion he had ignited so effortlessly continued to flow through her body.

One thing was certain: having Maxim by her side throughout the ceremony was not going to calm her nerves one bit.

'*Ta femme est très belle, Maxim.*'

At his estate manager and best man Victor's whispered compliment, Maxim shifted round from his position at the front of the church to glance over his shoulder.

The soaring strings of Pachelbel's *Canon in D*, which had been picked by the wedding organiser he had hired at great expense a week ago, filled the small chapel as Cara made her way down the aisle on Marcel Caron's arm to the hushed reverence of the crowd.

He stood, transfixed. His bride had her head

bent, watching her steps in the golden slippers, the simple but supremely elegant silk dress she wore shifting colour from gold to rose in the flickering glow of a thousand candles. Her blonde hair had been arranged in a pile of unruly curls threaded through with blue flowers to match her eyes. She wore no veil.

The air gathered in his lungs, threatening to strangle him as heat rose through his body like wildfire—the surge of pride and possessiveness like a tidal wave.

Mine.

The word echoed in his head again, unbidden, as it had on their first night together.

He tried to qualify and control it—the way he'd been trying to do for over a week. Ever since he'd left her in London. The wedding had been a necessary charade, for his business, the press and his personal standing in the community.

But as his eyes devoured the stunning woman walking towards him, it was hard to stick to the script he had written so carefully for himself when making the arrangements.

He noticed her knuckles whitening where she gripped the elaborate bouquet in her fist and realised that while Victor was correct—his wife was indeed exquisitely beautiful—she was also extremely nervous.

He tried to calm his breathing, finally forced to

admit that his insistence on this ceremony was not quite as pragmatic as he had wanted to believe.

He'd had no hand in choosing the dress, but as Cara approached him he realised he was glad the couturier had made no attempt to disguise her pregnancy. The child was a fact. A fact neither one of them could ignore. So why deny the strange surge of pride and possessiveness at the evidence that she was his?

While he had not wanted the affidavit he had signed to become public all those months ago, he couldn't deny he was pleased that everyone would know she had been untouched by his father. That while the old bastard had married her first, he had never known the pleasures of her beautiful body.

Perhaps the crowd would think her pregnancy was the only reason *he* had married her, and until this moment he had been determined to convince himself of the same. But as Cara's head finally lifted and her shy gaze met his, he was forced to acknowledge the basic biological urge to claim her he had never been able to contain.

Mine.

Marcel presented Cara's trembling hand to him as they drew level. Maxim captured her fingers in a firm grip and lifted them to his lips. He buzzed a kiss across her knuckles and whispered above the fading music, 'Do not fear, Cara. This will soon be over and then we can schedule the sex.'

It was supposed to be a joke, a poor attempt to ease the tension, but when the familiar blush ignited her cheeks—and the heat surged in his groin—the joke was on him.

He folded her arm under his and tucked her against his side to face the priest.

The cleric began to say the blessing—there would be no vows as those had already been made at the *mairie* in Auxerre. But Maxim barely heard the man's words, far too aware of Cara's body, ripe with his child, standing stiffly beside him as the cleric blessed their union before God, the local community and Maxim's employees and friends.

This marriage would be over once the child was born. He could never give her more. His panicked reaction to seeing his son ten days ago was all the proof he needed of that. But as they stood together in the candlelight, the eyes of everyone who mattered in his life upon them, the pressure in his chest refused to go away.

As the blessing finished and the priest gave him permission to kiss his bride, the primitive urge charged through his bloodstream like a living, breathing thing.

As he gathered Cara's lush body into his arms and conquered her lips in a searing, incendiary kiss, their audience and the reasons for the ceremony faded from his consciousness. All he could smell was her light flowery scent and the musk of her arousal, all he could comprehend was the feel of her soft, pliant, responsive body surrendering to his.

And all he wanted to do was brand her as his in the most basic way imaginable, as soon as was humanly possible.

CHAPTER THIRTEEN

'YOU MADE a very beautiful bride, *madame.*'

'Thank you, Antoinette,' Cara murmured as she watched her new maid pluck the pins out that were holding her elaborate hairdo aloft.

She was tired, and grateful the festivities—or at least the festivities she was expected to participate in—were over. She sighed as the heavy locks of hair tumbled down.

'Would *madame* like me to run a bath?' Antoinette asked in her perfect English.

'That would be wonderful,' Cara replied, still unused to having anyone wait on her.

The battalion of stylists and beauty therapists who had arrived in her suite to prepare her for the wedding had done a spectacular job. At least she had looked the part of Maxim's sophisticated society bride. But the truth was she had been terrified as she'd walked down the aisle on Marcel Caron's arm, the hauntingly beautiful classical music, played expertly by a string and woodwind orchestra in the corner of the chapel, only making her feel like more of a fraud.

The dress had been so close-fitting no one could have missed her baby bump and, while she could never be ashamed of her pregnancy, she had felt as if she'd had a sign round her neck saying 'shotgun wedding'.

But when Maxim had gripped her hand and brought it to his lips, the fear of exposure had been replaced by a more visceral fear. In that second, as his gaze roamed over her, rich with appreciation, she had felt beautiful, and truly seen, for the first time in her life… And it had terrified her. Because it could not possibly be true.

But what terrified her more was how much she had wanted to look beautiful, for him.

She stared at herself in the mirror.

She couldn't go there, she mustn't. Because she knew what would happen if she allowed herself to think that if she changed who she was it would make a man like Maxim truly care for her. It wouldn't.

She'd tried to change before, with the foster families she'd stayed with. Even tried to change for her own father as a young child, after her mother's death, when she'd sensed he was going to leave her too… It didn't work, it never had.

She let out a guttering breath and heard Antoinette's carefree humming while she prepared the bath in the adjoining room.

For goodness' sake, lighten up, Cara.

Tonight was an elaborate show. Maxim had said so himself. She mustn't take it so seriously.

The heady scent of lavender and rose drifted into her bedroom from the bathroom, and she recognised the tune Antoinette was humming—the sensual melody from their first waltz.

More unhelpful memories flooded back, of the rest of the evening, the romance of the *château*'s Great Hall, illuminated by thousands of candles and sprays of hothouse flowers. And that waltz with Maxim, as he had banded his strong arms around her, gathered her close and led her effortlessly through the steps of the dance so she didn't stumble or fall.

The twist of panic in her belly tightened. How could he have managed to make her feel so cherished, so adored, when none of it was real?

Everything he had done had been for the benefit of their audience, so why hadn't it felt that way? Was she really so desperate for affection she could be fooled by romance and spectacle— and the glow of desire in his rich brown eyes?

She pushed the memories into the furthest reaches of her brain. She had to remain a realist, or she would be destroyed at the end of all this. The way she had been destroyed as a child.

She went to pick up the heavy silver brush on the dressing table and clashed fingers with Antoinette, who had returned from the bathroom.

The maid laughed. 'I can brush *madame*'s hair, if you would like?'

Cara smiled at the young woman in the mirror, who was so much more sophisticated than she was. 'Would it be okay if I did it myself?'

'Of course.' Antoinette smiled. 'Would you like me to leave you to bathe?'

Cara nodded, desperate to be alone as her gaze strayed to the large four-poster bed which dominated the bedroom. She needed to get her thoughts in order before… Well, before Maxim arrived tonight, assuming he was coming. The comment he had made when she'd reached him at the altar had sounded like a joke. So why couldn't she stop fixating on it…and wanting desperately for it to be real?

'Should I return to help you dress for your wedding night?' the maid asked boldly.

'I think I can handle that,' Cara murmured, almost choking on her embarrassment. 'But thank you so much for your help this evening, Antoinette.'

The maid grinned, making her look very young. 'You are welcome, *madame*. I think Monsieur Durand chose very well for his wife.'

Before leaving, Antoinette laid out a gossamer-thin piece of lace on the bed then added with a sparkle of humour, 'The *couturière* left this for you to wear tonight. But as Monsieur Durand did not take his eyes from you all evening, I do not think you will need it for very long.'

'Right…thanks, Antoinette.' Cara's blush incinerated her cheeks as the maid left. And the pulse of need between her thighs—which was always there—pounded even harder.

Brushing the last of the wild flowers out of her hair, she laid the brush on the dressing table with trembling fingers and headed towards the bathroom. A claw-foot tub stood in the centre of the lavish room, facing tall French windows which looked out over the dark fields of vines beyond the estate's gardens. Slipping off the robe, she climbed into the steamy, fragrant bathwater, but as she soaked tired muscles, trying to loosen the kinks caused by this overwhelming day, and the last overwhelming week and a half, the throbbing ache between her thighs strengthened and the panic intensified.

She had already lost too much of herself during tonight's events. If only she had more experience. Should she risk sleeping with Maxim? Was she even capable of denying herself that pleasure? And if he did come to her tonight, how did she remember that this marriage was one of convenience, not love?

* * *

Maxim tapped gently on the door to Cara's suite of rooms. No reply. Was she already asleep?

But as he contemplated returning to his own rooms across the hallway, the sensual tension that had been tormenting him throughout the day—ever since she'd stepped off his private jet that morning—clawed at his gut again.

He didn't feel rational, or focused. He felt desperate—driven by a craving stronger than he had ever known.

Every time he had got a lungful of her scent today, each time he'd seen the heat warm her cheeks when she'd glanced his way, the hunger for her had increased. Their first dance had been torture, as her body softened in his arms and she'd allowed him to lead her in the steps—while all the time he had been thinking of another dance he wished to lead her in.

Every single thing about his wife turned him on. But was that really so surprising?

He had searched for five long months to find her and then forced himself to leave her for ten days while preparations for their marriage were made. And during all that time he had dreamed about her continuously—sweaty erotic dreams which had turned his hunger into something more than it was ever meant to be.

He wasn't a man used to having to deny his

natural urges, and every one of them had been focused on Cara for months. And now she was his wife, was it any wonder he wanted to consummate their marriage? Surely they both deserved something more from this union than simply security for the child? Madame Moreau, the Parisian obstetrician he had hired, had confirmed what Dr Karim had said in London. Cara and the child were healthy; there was nothing to fear from sexual intercourse.

Damn it, stop second-guessing yourself. You can hardly satisfy this hunger from the hallway.

He knocked again, then tentatively opened the door, wondering if she was asleep. As he entered the room, the light coming from the bathroom illuminated the empty bed, and a scrap of something lacy and insubstantial laid upon it.

Just the sight of the negligee and the thought of Cara's full curves barely concealed by it had the heat surging into his groin.

He could hear splashing in the adjoining bathroom and smell the heady fragrance of flowers.

He cursed softly to himself then walked across the room, unable to resist the pull of a desire so strong it had been driving him crazy for hours, days, weeks…hell, even months.

He stood in the bathroom doorway to absorb the sight of his bride in the free-standing tub unobserved. Her heavy breasts were misted with moisture, while damp tendrils of hair clung to her high cheekbones.

He groaned.

Her head shot round, and what he saw in her eyes—stunned desire, naked need—echoed in his gut and turned the erection to throbbing iron. The emotion that gripped his chest felt like more than desire, more than passion, more than the basic urge to mate—he struggled to beat it back, to control it.

This was just hunger, nothing more, nothing less; it only felt like more because he desired her so much—and the fact of her pregnancy had resurrected emotions, vulnerabilities, that were best left buried.

'Maxim?' she said, folding her arms over her beautiful breasts to cover her nakedness. 'You're… You're here.'

He could hear the wariness in her voice, see the shyness in her flushed face. Damn, why did her innocence make her even more exquisite? It made no sense. He had always preferred the women he slept with to be bold and assertive, ready to tell him what they enjoyed, but, with Cara, her pleasure was like a rare gift waiting to be unwrapped. And, weirdly, her innocence made him feel untouched too, discovering the limits of his own pleasure for the first time.

The thought was so damn intoxicating he had to swallow another groan.

'Do you wish me to leave?' he asked, even though it was the hardest question he had ever asked. If she said yes, he would have to go, even though the thought of stepping away from the feast before his eyes might well tip him over the edge into insanity.

He saw her slender throat tighten as she swallowed, but then she shook her head.

He sent up a silent prayer of thanks to whoever might be watching over him in that moment. And sent up a silent vow too, that he would do his very best to treat her with the respect her inexperience—and her condition—deserved, even if the hunger clawing at his gut was already more than he could bear.

An idea sprung into his mind, erotic but also playful, and his erection stiffened even more.

'Would you like me to wash your back?' he asked, trying to keep his voice light, the opposite of what he felt.

'Um…' She chewed her lip, considering, and every one of his pulse points throbbed in agony, waiting for her decision. 'That would be nice, if you're sure you want to.'

He masked the inevitable groan with a husky half laugh. She was going to kill him before the night was out. '*J'en suis certain*, Cara.'

He sat down on the gilded chair in the corner of the room to unlace his shoes and had managed to strip off his shirt and tuxedo trousers before her shocked voice asked, 'Maxim, what are you doing?'

'Joining you in the bath,' he said as he lowered his boxer shorts and watched her gaze drop to the painful erection. Stunned need—and panic—flared in the blue depths and he laughed again, the sound considerably more tortured this time. 'It's the only way to do a thorough job.'

She didn't take her eyes off the mammoth erection as he crossed the room. He climbed in behind her, the water rising to lap over the lip of the tub as he sunk down, his erection now snug against her bottom. She trembled, and moved, instinctively rubbing against the stiff length.

Oui, she was definitely going to kill him, but at least he would die in a state of bliss.

He reached past her to pluck the soap from the side of the tub. He lathered his hands, then placed them on her shoulders. Beginning at her nape, he worked down her spine as far as he could reach, kneading the tight muscles, glad when the sinews began to loosen under his thumbs. She still had her arms clasped across her chest, but he could feel the tension gradually releasing. At last her arms softened enough for him to draw them down.

He covered her breasts with his hands, and leant over her shoulder to watch the nipples— rosy from the water—elongate under his focused caresses.

'Maxim, I… That's not my back…' Her voice broke on the husky comment, the raw need in her tone a potent aphrodisiac.

'Yes, but I feel they need my attention,' he teased, desperately trying to keep the mood playful. 'It's my job as your husband to make sure you are properly washed.'

'It… It is?' she said, her body relaxing enough to lean into him.

Unable to bear the tension any longer, he leaned over her shoulder and, holding the heavy weight of her breasts in his palms, whispered in her ear, 'Turn your head for me, *ma femme*.'

She did as he asked, and he claimed her lips. The angle was too awkward to go deep, but even so her tongue tangled with his, meeting his shallow thrusts. He lifted his head first, her soft sigh of disappointment like a siren call to his senses. Standing, he lifted her from the water and stepped out of the tub with her in his arms.

'Maxim, be careful, you might slip,' she said, gripping his shoulders.

He placed a kiss on her nose, pink and delicious, and laughed at her practicality.

Dieu, could she be any more exquisite?

He brushed his feet on the damp bath mat and strode into the adjoining bedroom with her held high in his arms. 'Take a towel,' he said as they walked past the pile on the bathroom dresser.

Placing her on her feet beside the four-poster bed, he took the fluffy bath sheet from her and proceeded to dry her wild tumble of curls, then her body, taking the opportunity to run the soft towelling over her flushed fragrant flesh, marvelling at the changes—surprised by how much they aroused him.

He would not have believed he could want her more than he had that first night. But he did. Her breasts were fuller and firmer, her curves more lush where her body had ripened in pregnancy.

Was she more sensitive? he wondered.

Sinking to his knees, he discarded the towel and gripped her hips, suddenly desperate to taste her.

'Maxim!' She grasped his shoulders, her whole body trembling as if she were in a high wind. He knew how she felt, every inch of his skin was alive and raring to devour her, the erection so hard it hurt.

'What are you doing?' she said.

He looked up and smiled at the stunned desire in her face. He ran his fingers over the seam of her sex—and decided to taste her another time.

If he feasted on her tonight he might not be able to hold onto the frenzy building in his blood.

'Making sure you are ready for me,' he said, exploring the swollen folds.

She jolted and moaned as his thumb stroked across the slick nub of her clitoris. 'I'm… I'm very ready,' she said.

'*Bien*.' He stood and licked his fingertips then watched her pupils expand. He'd done his best to take this slowly, to woo her, but he couldn't hold back much longer. Despite the need rioting through his system, though, he took in the firm mound of her belly—aware of the life that grew inside her.

'Climb onto the bed, Cara, on all fours,' he managed, his voice raw, as violent need sparked along his nerve-endings.

She seemed confused, so he took her elbow and guided her onto the bed, then rolled her over gently and lifted her hips. The lips of her sex quivered, swollen and shiny with her juices. He placed himself at her entrance, the sight of the thick erection entering her so erotic he felt dazed.

He slid deep in one slow, careful thrust, filling her to the hilt. Her muscles clenched around him, tighter than a fist, her shocked sob making his erection grow to impossible proportions.

He began to move, rocking his hips, out and

back, to claim every centimetre of her sex. This part of her, at least, still belonged to him.

But as he plunged deep, took more, branded her as his…the words of the ceremony in the *mairie* that afternoon—words which shouldn't have meant anything—poured through his mind all over again, this time binding, and true. Too true.

Her sex clenched around him in orgasm, massaging his length and triggering his own titanic climax. A shout was wrenched from his throat as his seed emptied inside her.

But as they shuddered through the devastating orgasm together, a disturbing thought occurred to him. She was his, but only until the child was born, so why did this need feel too huge to ever be sated?

CHAPTER FOURTEEN

CARA AWOKE THE next morning to find the light shining through open shutters… And the bed beside her empty.

She'd tried to convince herself last night, as the afterglow had suffused her senses and Maxim had held her while she fell asleep, that all her fanciful feelings about him, about her marriage, were just endorphins. An industrial-strength hormonal rush which had only become more potent because of her pregnancy. Her feelings for Maxim, for this marriage, were nothing to be terrified of, because they were just a chemical reaction she couldn't control.

But as she stretched in the bed alone, the luxury linen sheets like sandpaper on her over-sensitive skin, she couldn't help fixating on the empty space beside her, and struggled to explain away the tenderness beating under her ribs. And the wave of disappointment… And longing.

Or the questions that bombarded her.

Where had he gone? Had he returned to his own rooms? Why hadn't he stayed?

She pushed the questions back, tried to stop the tender spot in her chest becoming the hollow ache of inadequacy that had defined her childhood as she slipped out of bed and walked into the bathroom on unsteady legs.

The damp bath mat had been hooked over the heated towel rail and the bath had been emptied. Even so, the erotic memories from yesterday evening, his tender ministrations as he'd joined her in the bath and the powerful, passionate sex that had followed assailed her senses again. But as she searched the room for Maxim's clothes, or any sign that he had ever been there, her confidence faded.

After taking a quick shower, she managed to find a pair of designer jeans and a pretty blue blouse in the wardrobe full of expensive new clothes in the suite's dressing room.

She could hear the bustle of activity downstairs as she stepped onto the landing. The clean-up operation was in full swing. After wandering downstairs unobserved, she headed past the Great Hall and saw a small army of staff, busy packing away the remnants of last night's wedding banquet.

The show was well and truly over.

She spotted Antoinette amid the mêlée.

'Antoinette, *bonjour*!' she called out, glad of

the distraction. While she had no aptitude for social events, she knew a lot about housekeeping. And cleaning. Perhaps she could help? And it would take her mind off last night, and Maxim's absence from her bed this morning.

Antoinette rushed over, looking concerned. '*Madame*, I am so sorry. Monsieur Durand gave us instructions not to wake you.'

'It's okay. I'm an early riser.'

'We did not expect you to be up so early. I am so sorry I didn't attend you immediately.'

'That's quite all right, Antoinette, really,' Cara said, feeling a blush work up her neck on cue. Did everyone know what they'd been doing last night? 'Do you know where Monsieur Durand is?' she asked, feeling a little foolish.

Antoinette nodded enthusiastically. 'Monsieur Durand is in the breakfast room.'

The maid led her through the house, leaving her at the entrance to a huge glass conservatory. The lush planting inside the room contrasted with the bare wintery gardens shrouded in an early morning mist outside. She walked through the foliage, and spied Maxim seated at an ornate iron table in a picturesque alcove, sipping coffee and reading something on his phone.

Her husband. Her lover.

The emotions she'd worked so hard to control

during the night rushed towards her again like a tidal wave, threatening to knock her off her feet.

How could they be even stronger now and more volatile? And what was she supposed to do to make them stop?

Dressed in a crisp white shirt, his jaw clean-shaven and his hair recently brushed, his gaze was locked on the screen. With the flaky remnants of his breakfast on the plate in front of him, Maxim looked focused, alert, confident and every inch the captain of industry.

She cleared her throat and his gaze rose from his phone. Passion flared in his eyes but, before she could respond to it, he frowned.

'Cara, why are you awake so early?' he said, not sounding pleased to see her. 'After last night, you need your sleep.'

All her questions about what time he'd left her and where he planned to sleep in the future died on her tongue. It wasn't exactly a reprimand, but it was close enough. Heat flushed through her at the mention of 'last night' but she forced herself to walk towards him.

'It's not *that* early,' she said in her defence.

He stood and pulled out a chair. 'Sit,' he said, placing a perfunctory kiss on her cheek as he tucked the chair in. He seemed distracted but the buzz of his lips still set off a shiver of reaction. She tried not to dwell on it. Her response to him was physical not emotional. Why couldn't she remember that?

'What would you like to eat? I will have the chef prepare it for you,' he said, sitting down.

'I'm... I'm not that hungry,' she said.

'Cara—' his brows furrowed '—you must eat.'

She nodded, remembering his obsession with her health and where it came from. 'A croissant then, I guess.'

'That is not enough,' he said, then lifted the phone and barked an order for an array of breakfast dishes.

'I'm not sure I can eat all that,' she said when he ended the call to the kitchen.

He didn't seem too pleased with that response, but simply nodded. 'There is an app on the phone Jean-Claude supplied you with. It has a direct link to the staff. If there is anything you require, just let them know. I have hired a nutritionist to suggest meals suitable for pregnant women, you can consult with her, also through the app.'

'Okay.' She wanted to be pleased with his thoughtfulness, but instead she felt overwhelmed again. And a little frustrated. Where was the man who had made such passionate and provocative love to her last night? And where was the woman who had made that commanding, confident man moan?

She didn't feel powerful any more, she felt inadequate and out of place—the way she had so many times before when she'd arrived at a new foster home, desperate to fit in, to find a place for herself. Only to discover there wasn't one.

'It is good you are here,' he said, surprising her, but, just as her heart lifted at the encouraging statement, he added, 'I am about to head to the winery for the day.'

'But it's Sunday!' she heard herself say. *And it's our honeymoon*, she almost added, but managed to stop herself—after all, this wasn't a real marriage.

But, even so, his imminent departure made her feel strangely bereft. She'd hoped to have a chance to talk to him this morning, to get to know him better and maybe discuss her role at the *château*. Was there anything he needed her to do as his wife? She wanted to be useful.

He smiled indulgently. 'Yes, but unfortunately the vines do not respect weekends.'

'When will you be back?'

'This evening. Do not wait up for me, I may be late.'

'Okay,' Cara replied, trying hard not to feel abandoned.

Why was she being so ridiculous? This marriage wasn't real, however real it had seemed last night.

'By the way,' Maxim continued, wiping his

mouth with his napkin, 'I will be travelling to Tuscany for a week in March. I will need you to join me at the end of the trip to attend a ball being held in honour of the man who, I hope, will be selling his vineyards to me.'

A spike of anxiety at the thought that he was going to leave her for a whole week sent her thoughts into a tailspin. 'A ball?'

'Yes. Jean-Claude will make all the arrangements and the *couturière* has been asked to supply suitable clothing,' he murmured.

His hand covered hers on the table. The warmth of his rough palm sent the familiar desire sprinting up her arm to tighten her nipples. 'Do not panic, Cara, you have a few weeks to prepare.' He squeezed her fingers and lifted them to his mouth. The press of his lips and his teasing smile had her heart doing a jitterbug in her chest.

'I enjoyed last night immensely,' he said, the rough intimacy in his voice stroking her senses. 'Would you like me to come to your rooms tonight, if it is not too late when I return from the winery?'

'I... Yes, that would be...' She swallowed. What? Fun? Wonderful? Exciting? All of those things and more? 'I would like that very much,' she managed, disturbed not just by her instant, instinctive response to him—and her complete inability to say no—but also by how much she was already looking forward to his visit.

When he released her hand, she clasped her fingers in her lap.

How did he do that? How did he disturb her and excite her at one and the same time? Was this need inside her normal? She'd tried to persuade herself it was last night, but if her response to him was just about endorphins, why did she feel so empty inside at the thought of not seeing him all day?

'Is there anything you'd like me to do today?' she asked.

His frown reappeared. '*Do?*' he asked, clearly confused.

'I mean, as your wife?' she said. If she kept busy, surely it would help to alleviate the hollow feeling of inadequacy. 'I'd love to be useful.'

She certainly didn't want to sit around all day doing nothing, or she was likely to spend too much time dwelling on this marriage that wasn't a real marriage, and how much she was going to miss her husband who wasn't a real husband.

Maxim huffed out an incredulous laugh. 'There is nothing for you to do, Cara. You are my wife. The staff are here to wait on you. Not the other way around.'

As if on cue, a parade of footmen arrived to deliver the breakfast Maxim had ordered for her.

An array of food, enough to feed several people, was laid out on the breakfast table. Plates filled with buttery pastries, fresh fruit, a selection of bread and cheese and even a fluffy omelette were revealed with a flourish before the staff bowed and left. Fragrant scents filled the room and made her stomach growl.

'*Bon appétit*.' Maxim smiled then stood as he glanced at his watch. 'I must go. Hopefully I will see you tonight,' he said, leaning down to give her a kiss on the cheek. 'Eat,' he said. 'You need food.' Her heart squeezed and her stomach knotted at the casual reference to her welfare. Was he thinking of the child too, as well as her? 'And do not concern yourself with unnecessary chores.' His lips skimmed down to her earlobe. The nip of his teeth had a shuddering sigh issuing from her lips. He laughed, the husky sound reverberating in her sex. 'You will need your rest—I intend to keep you very busy when I return.'

Before she had a chance to gather her thoughts again, he was gone.

She forced herself to tuck into the delicious omelette, knowing he was right about her nutrition, and tried to control a pang of melancholy. But as she devoured the delicious food, much hungrier than she'd realised, a plan formed.

Maxim hadn't said she *couldn't* find a role for herself here. He'd simply said she didn't need to.

Keeping busy, having a role, had been her way to cope with the constant feelings of isolation she'd experienced as a child.

After finishing the omelette and most of the fresh fruit, she headed off to find Antoinette.

She hated confrontations, but she didn't need to get Maxim's permission to figure out her role here for the next few months. Ultimately, it was up to her to decide what being Maxim Durand's wife meant, because she was the new *temporary* mistress of Château Durand, not him.

CHAPTER FIFTEEN

'YOUR WIFE IS exquisite, Durand.'

'Hmm…' Maxim barely registered his business rival Giovanni Romano's observation, thanks to the blood pumping through his body at breakneck speed ever since Cara had arrived at the Donati Ball half an hour ago.

He'd made a point of not leaving Donati's palazzo to collect her from their nearby hotel when he had been informed she had arrived in Italy, knowing if he saw her before the event, in a bedroom, after seven days—and nights—of separation, they would probably end up missing the ball altogether.

She looked stunning in a shimmering blue satin gown, her figure even more lush and gorgeous than when he had left Burgundy a week ago for this business trip; her blonde curls were artfully arranged with diamond pins which sparkled in the overhead light of the chandelier. He had not been able to take his gaze off her since he'd greeted her.

They had been married now for nearly a month. She had settled into life at the *château* with surprising ease. While he had not been pleased with her decision to befriend his staff, and take on the domestic duties of the mistress of the *château*, he had been forced to accept she needed something to keep her busy or she would be bored. His wife, he had discovered, had a prodigious work ethic and was incapable of being idle.

So he had indulged her, on the understanding that she would not take on any tasks that required physical labour. He had also had Jean-Claude send a confidential email to the *château*'s staff without Cara's knowledge, telling them they would be fired if they allowed her to do anything more strenuous than lift a teapot.

Over the weeks he had begun to notice her presence in ways he had not expected—little touches, small changes that made the house more charming, more welcoming, more liveable—the bunches of fresh flowers that had begun to appear as spring bloomed over the estate, the smiles of the staff, who all seemed to adore her, and the smooth running of the household which allowed him to concentrate on his business instead of having to waste time making domestic decisions that didn't interest him.

And the sex each night, when he returned from work, continued to be addictive.

In fact, he had become so eager to see her each night, and so reluctant to leave every morning, it had begun to make him feel extremely uneasy. He'd promised himself after their wedding night that he would not spend the whole night with her, but each time he went to her bed he found it harder and harder to leave.

He'd planned this trip precisely so he could break the habit of keeping her in his arms until daybreak—and begin to re-establish the distance between them that a month of marriage had eroded.

He stared at Cara, standing a few feet away at the elaborate buffet, talking to Donati's elegantly dressed seventy-five-year-old wife, and was forced to admit that his plan had failed miserably. She looked so luminous to him, she was practically glowing.

Anticipation thrummed through his system like an electrical charge. Tonight was important to his business. Tomorrow he was supposed to be sealing the deal with Eduardo Donati and beating out Romano to the best vineyards in Tuscany—and completing Durand's expansion into the Italian market—but he couldn't concentrate on anything, because all he could think about was taking his wife into his arms and making her sigh and moan and beg.

She was like a drug he was finding it increasingly hard to live without. He'd torn himself away from her for seven days to control his obsession with her and it had done exactly the opposite. All he'd been able to think about in the past week was her.

All he'd dreamt about was her. And not just sexual dreams, but more disturbing ones—dominated by the vision of her eyes filled with compassion the day they'd first met, the feel of her exhausted in his arms when he had carried her away from the Valentine's Ball in London, the joy on her face when they had sat together in the Harley Street clinic and seen their son for the first time, the open smile that spread across her features each night when he arrived in her bedroom.

How had he become so attuned to even the most subtle of her reactions? He always tried to be considerate with the women he dated, but with Cara it was more than that. Every one of his senses was more focused, more alert, more desperate if he was near her, and now, he'd discovered, also when he was not.

No woman had ever distracted him from his business before now. But it was taking every ounce of his control not to stalk towards her, scoop her up and march out of this godforsaken event so he could take her somewhere private and relieve the insistent craving to have her again.

Apparently seven days of denial—during which he'd forced himself not to contact her—had only increased his addiction.

'Pregnancy suits her—when is the child due?'

Maxim turned at Romano's wry observation, his temper spiking at the man's mocking smile. He'd had to force himself to leave Cara's side five minutes ago—to calm his racing heartbeat—and had been waylaid on the way back from the restroom by Romano. The last damn person he wanted to speak to.

'In the summer,' he said. The twist of anxiety that thoughts of the child usually brought with it sharpened.

He had married Cara to keep her safe, and give his son a name, but every time he thought about the baby now, the guilty weight in his stomach seemed to become heavier. The fierce protective instinct he could not contain had begun to torture him every time he thought of the child growing inside her, and then his mother's face—the last time he had seen it—would swim into his mind's eye.

'Ne me quitte pas, Maxim.'

He cut off the debilitating memory. Again.

The same memory that had first assailed him in the ultrasound suite, and then returned when he had left Cara's bed on their wedding night—sated, exhausted and yet still aroused.

He had understood, as he'd cleared away the evidence of their night together in the bathroom, desperate to return to her bed and hold her throughout the night, that he couldn't allow such a foolish indulgence. So why hadn't he been able to stick to his promise?

The novelty value of sex with Cara, sex with his wife, had made their physical relationship more intense than any he had ever experienced. But he must not let that blind him to the limitations of this marriage, for Cara's sake as well as his own.

He could not let her become dependent on him. The way his mother had been. Or he would fail her too.

'You don't sound too pleased about the prospect of fatherhood,' Romano said, still with that wry mocking grin on his face. 'Although I take it the pregnancy was planned?'

'And this would be your business, how exactly?' Maxim planted his fists firmly in his pockets, resisting the urge to knock the smug smile off Romano's face.

Flattening the bastard at Donati's eightieth birthday ball would defeat the purpose of the whole trip—namely to earn the old vintner's trust so he would sell him the legendary Donati vines.

'So you don't deny it?' Romano laughed, the sound rough with contempt. 'I have to admire your dedication to the vines, Durand.'

'What are you talking about?' Maxim snapped, the control he had always been so proud of fraying dangerously at the edges. He wasn't a thug, a gangster, an ill-bred upstart, as so many people had claimed when he had first had the audacity to enter the wine trade—he had ignored all those insults, determined not to live up to people's low expectations, or his own father's scorn, but Romano's attitude was starting to irritate him. Big time.

'Oh, I think you know,' Romano said, the smug twist of his lips enough to send Maxim's temper into a tailspin.

'Really?' Maxim's hands shot out to grab the lapels of Romano's dinner jacket and haul him forward until they were nose to nose. 'I think you should spell it out.'

He ground the words out, not caring about the gasps of the nearby guests, who had shuffled back to give them room for their altercation.

'All I'm saying is impregnating old man de la Mare's hot little widow before the guy was even cold in his grave was a smart, and I'm sure very enjoyable, way to get his land.'

Romano's accusation sliced through the last frayed threads of Maxim's control like a rusty blade. His fist shot out and connected with Romano's jaw, the shudder of pain in his knuckles worth it as the man flew backwards and landed on his backside with a thud.

'Don't ever talk about my wife again,' Maxim growled as he flexed his fingers, ignoring the shocked gasps of their audience and the sight of one woman fainting into the arms of her partner.

The red mist of rage refused to clear as he watched Romano jiggle his jaw. 'Good right hook, Durand,' the man said as he laughed.

'Durand? What is going on?' Donati's horrified shout did nothing to calm Maxim's raging heartbeat or the fury pounding through his veins at Romano's insult. The man had insinuated that Maxim was a whore but, worse than that, he had implied that Cara was a whore too. A woman who had been innocent until he had touched her.

'Maxim, is everything okay?' Cara's concerned voice seemed to tether him to reality as she gripped the sleeve of his jacket.

He turned to see her face, sweet, worried, compassionate. The red mist cleared, to be replaced by something even more disturbing. Grasping her cheeks, he kissed her, the meeting of their lips making her soften instinctively. The heady rush of blood to his groin drowned out the indignant whispers of the crowd, and Donati's threats to cancel the sale.

Lifting his head, he grasped her hand. They needed to get out of here so he could feed the hunger that would not stop.

He turned to Donati. 'We're leaving. If you want to sell to Romano instead, that is your decision, Eduardo. But no one insults my wife.'

He marched out of the ballroom towards his waiting car, with Cara's hand gripped in his. She stumbled and he stopped, to scoop her into his arms. The crowd parted before him like the Red Sea before Moses, the whispers of outrage only feeding the adrenaline rush.

Damn them.

He didn't care. He couldn't wait, couldn't stop—he needed her. The desperation intensified as her body softened against his and her scent filled his senses. The way he had dreamed of for seven long nights and every day he had spent away from her.

'Maxim, what did Mr Romano say?' Cara asked as she clung to her husband's neck and tried to ignore the people gaping at them as Maxim carried her out of the ballroom and down the wide sweeping staircase to the palazzo's entrance.

The truth was she'd known something was wrong as soon as she'd arrived at the ball. Maxim had been on edge, curt and annoyed, the intensity in him even more pronounced than usual.

She'd tried to swallow her unease. She'd been disappointed that he hadn't been waiting for her when she'd arrived at the lavish hilltop hotel in Tuscany three hours ago. Instead there had been the familiar battalion of beauty therapists and a stylist waiting to dress her for the ball, and a lonely drive in a limousine—while she chewed on her newly manicured nails—before Maxim had greeted her at the palazzo's entrance then whisked her inside to introduce her as his wife.

While the usual rush of endorphins had assailed her as soon as his hand had settled on the small of her back, and his fierce gaze had darkened as it roamed over her, she'd felt like a decoration, an accessory, as he'd introduced her to an array of people she didn't know.

If only he'd contacted her during the last seven days, told her something about the event, she might have been able to get involved in the conversation, and control her nerves.

It had been a struggle not to feel inadequate, or invisible. Or confused again about her place in his life. She'd worked so hard in the last three weeks to be useful at the *château*—and she'd managed it, despite Maxim's initial objections.

She'd come to love her 'work' as the mistress of Château Durand. Here, at last, was something she could do to help Maxim. Something she was good at.

Maybe Maxim had never said that he appreciated her input. Perhaps he didn't even notice the changes she'd made—he spent very little time at the *château* after all. But she noticed, and it made her happy—which was why tonight had felt like a step back.

And now he'd hit a man.

'That bastard insulted you.' Maxim bit the words out as he marched out of the palazzo's main entrance and demanded his car be brought round by the wide-eyed doorman. The limousine whisked to a stop in front of them moments later.

'What did he say?' she said, confused, not just by the searing comment itself but by the inappropriate flutter of something in her chest at the thought that Maxim had punched a man to defend her honour. 'He doesn't even know me.'

Maxim let her down but, before she had a chance to climb into the car and escape the stares of the staff still watching from the *palazzo*'s entrance, Maxim grasped her hips and pulled her into his embrace.

'It doesn't matter, he won't be repeating it,' he said, before covering her mouth with his.

The kiss was firm and hungry, devouring her gasp of surprise. His hands roamed over the bare skin of her back and sent her senses reeling. As always, she reacted instinctively, the flutter turning into a vibrant hum as she kissed him back like a starving woman.

This, at least, was something she understood, something she knew how to do.

He groaned, and ripped his mouth away. 'Get in the car. I can't wait much longer to have you.'

The urgency in his voice, and the desire flaring in his eyes, sent her senses into overdrive. She scrambled in.

'Take us to the Castillo. And don't disturb us,' he said to the driver, before pressing the button to raise the privacy screen, plunging them into shadows.

The car drove off into the night.

She could hear her own breathing, and his, before he reached for her and dragged her across his lap. She straddled him, her hands gripping his strong shoulders, trying to find purchase as the giddy rush of emotion—that he needed her so much—threatened to overwhelm her.

Her thighs quivered as his strong hands skimmed up her bare legs, lifting the gown to the waist.

'Release me, Cara,' he demanded as his fingers found the lace gusset of her panties and sunk beneath to torture the molten spot with his thumb.

She bucked against the delicious torment, fumbling with his fly in the darkness, her hands clumsy with need. Her body was already on the edge of the familiar precipice. At last she found the tab and eased it down, then captured his solid length in her hand.

He moaned, the guttural sound like a benediction. The desire to take him into her mouth—the way she knew he loved—was overwhelming but, as she edged back to give herself room, his hands clamped on her hips, preventing her.

'No, Cara, not like that, not tonight. Tonight I need to be inside you.'

She nodded, unable to speak, desperate now too.

The shocking sound of ripping lace barely registered as he tore away the last impediment to their joining, then lifted her hips to lower her onto the rampant erection.

His size and girth stretched her as he impaled her, making her shudder. She clung to him, her nails digging into the fabric of his tuxedo jacket as she tried to control the waves already threatening to annihilate her.

It was too much and yet not enough.

Holding her hips, he began to move her on the huge erection, guiding her to ride him in a slow, sensuous, all-consuming rhythm.

Their pants misted the car's windows, the hum of the engine vibrating through her as the waves of release crashed over her and then receded to build again…

She couldn't take any more, her body battered and bowed, another orgasm hurtling towards her. Freeing her breast from the satin, his mouth found her engorged nipple and suckled hard.

The strong drawing sensation sent her crashing over again. She collapsed on top of him, a sweaty heap as his roar of completion echoed in her ear.

She came down slowly, spent and exhausted and raw, as she struggled to contain the familiar rush of emotion.

But, just as she attempted to lift herself free, she felt the little dig inside her body of their baby, making its presence felt. She clasped her belly, and his whole body tensed.

'You are okay?' he murmured in the darkness, sounding stricken.

'Yes, it's… The baby moved, that's all.'

He lifted her gently off him, carefully pulled up the bodice of her gown to cover her exposed breast. It was only then that she realised the car had stopped moving.

She adjusted her gown, painfully aware of her husband's sudden withdrawal as the lights of the Castillo Hotel flickered through the misted windows.

He tapped on the partition. 'We are ready to disembark.'

The driver opened her door seconds later and helped her out, keeping his eyes downcast. Had he guessed what they had been doing? He must have done.

But somehow she didn't care. Why should they be ashamed of their need?

Maxim got out of his side of the car, then strode round to capture her hand. He led her into the hotel. They travelled in silence in the lift. What had happened? Why did she feel bereft, unable to bridge the gap between them? How could the sex be so intense and yet change nothing?

As they approached the door to the suite, he dropped her hand. 'I will see you at the estate in a few days' time.'

She clasped her arms over her bosom, her nipple still raw, the hum of sensation from their frantic lovemaking still *there* in her sex. 'You're not... You're not coming in?' she asked.

'I have my own suite,' he said.

The news was like a blow. She had assumed, had hoped, that tonight they would be sharing a bedroom... And that Maxim would wake up with her in the morning.

Maxim always left her rooms after their lovemaking, but she knew it had become more and more of a struggle for him. Each night he had held her longer and waited longer to leave. And she had rejoiced at this sign of progress. But why had she deluded herself that tonight would be the first night they would spend the whole night together when he hadn't even bothered to call in the last seven days?

'Maxim, wait,' she said, gripping his arm. 'Did I... Did I do something wrong tonight?'

He pressed a finger to her lips, his expression no longer blank but filled with regret. 'Shh, Cara, you were exquisite. You are the perfect wife.'

If that were so, why did she feel like even less of a wife than she had a week ago? She gulped down the fear expanding in her throat. And forced herself to ask the question that was torturing her. 'Then why don't you want to stay in my bed for a whole night?'

'I cannot stay.' He cupped her cheek, stroked his thumb across the sensitive flesh, tender from the rub of his stubble. 'If I did, I would exhaust you and the baby.'

It was an excuse he had used before, to leave her bed at dawn, and she'd never challenged it because she knew where his fears about her safety came from. But this time the truth spilled out of her mouth, regardless.

'You wouldn't exhaust us.' She gathered every last ounce of her courage. 'I'm fit and healthy and so is our baby.'

His gaze dipped to her stomach, prominently displayed in the close-fitting gown. Had the baby's movement spooked him? But he didn't look spooked, just distant. And suddenly so aloof.

'You need your rest,' he continued before she had a chance to gather her wits and question him more. 'You must travel back to Château Durand alone tomorrow.'

'You're not returning home with me?' she blurted out, the panic twisting into something more painful.

His eyebrow quirked at the mention of the word *home* and she realised Maxim still didn't see the *château* as a home, even though she had tried so hard to make it one.

'I need to repair the deal with Donati, if I can. If not, I have other business in the Loire before I return. But I should see you in a few days.'

He lifted her numb fingers and buzzed a kiss across the knuckles. The stupidly gallant gesture made her want to cry.

He'd made no promises, and she had no doubt at all that he wouldn't contact her before he returned. But somehow it wasn't enough any more.

'*Au revoir*, Cara,' he murmured, before leaving her standing in the doorway to her suite.

She watched him go, his broad shoulders stretching the seams of his suit jacket. A jacket she had gripped for dear life only minutes ago, while he took her apart with his lovemaking.

But it wasn't lovemaking, she thought as she stepped into the suite and closed the door. Not for him.

How many times had she been rejected in her life? So why should this rejection hurt so much more?

She leant against the door, blinking back the stinging sensation in her eyes and swallowed around the tightness in her throat as she finally acknowledged the truth she had been denying for weeks—every time Maxim took her with such passion, every time he stayed a little bit longer in her bed, every time he smiled at her, his eyes dark with approval, every time he frowned, concerned for her well-being or that of the baby...

She had fallen hopelessly in love with her temporary husband.

She pushed away from the door, kicked off her shoes, walked into the lavish bedroom and gazed at the four-poster bed where she would sleep alone tonight, while her husband slept alone down the hallway.

She was scared, terrified really, of her feelings for him. But as she lay down on the empty bed, inhaled the smell of him still clinging to her skin, she wondered...

What if Maxim were running scared too, of his feelings for her?

She rolled onto her side and curled up into a tight ball to cradle the precious bump of her pregnancy.

When Maxim returned to the *château* she had

to find a way to confront him, to show him how she felt. And somehow, eventually, she had to find the courage to demand from Maxim something she had believed she could never have, never deserve, ever since her father's desertion all those years ago. His love.

It was a risk, a huge risk. If she failed, she would feel like that abandoned child again, alone and unlovable. But if she succeeded? Her heart lifted into her throat. *If* she succeeded, perhaps she could finally let go of that girl for ever and have Maxim's heart, as well as his body.

CHAPTER SIXTEEN

'WHERE SHALL WE put this bunch?' Antoinette asked, her eyes bright with excitement.

Cara grinned back, feeling like a naughty schoolgirl with a secret. Not that she'd ever been naughty as a schoolgirl, she'd always been too scared that if she caused any trouble her latest foster family would chuck her back into the system.

But she wasn't that insecure child any more, she thought staunchly as she grasped the ribbon on the bunch of gold-and-silver balloons Antoinette and two of the estate's footmen had been helping her blow up to decorate the dining room.

Maybe part of that child still lived inside her, she would have done something like this a lot sooner if she didn't. But it was way past time she put that child aside.

'Move the ladder and I'll put them up there,' she said, pointing at the cornice above the table she and Antoinette had laid out that morning.

Maxim was due back in less than an hour. He'd stayed away for a whole week in the end, supposedly to repair the deal with Donati. But in a way she was glad, because now she was sure she had been right to think he was running scared too. And right to know she couldn't let him do that any more.

Cara swallowed around the ball of anticipation—and fear—lodged in her throat. His absence had given her a chance to muster her courage but, more than that, it had also, completely by chance, gifted her with the perfect way to show him how much she felt for him.

'Is everything okay, *madame*?' Antoinette asked.

'Yes.' Cara smiled at the maid, determined to believe it as she tied off the ribbon on the balloons and climbed the ladder.

Maxim was a workaholic, who had an almost preternatural ability to focus on the now. She also knew, from what she knew of his past, that the reason he worked so hard was to overcome the deprivations of his childhood. She also suspected he was nervous about becoming a father. She understood that, because she was nervous about becoming a mother too. But shouldn't that give them an even better reason to forge a bond that went beyond sex?

'Be careful, *madame*,' Antoinette said as she steadied the ladder.

'I will be,' Cara said as she stretched to pin the balloons to the cornicing, her baby bump pressing against the metal.

She wanted this small celebration to be ready for Maxim's arrival. She knew he was unlikely to want a big fuss—he hadn't even mentioned to her that today was his birthday. But, as someone who had rarely had the chance to celebrate her own birthday, she suspected he had also missed out during his childhood. She knew his mother and he had been left living in abject poverty after Pierre had thrown them out when he was young. And she also knew he had left Burgundy at only fifteen to make his way in the wine trade. While her childhood had been blighted by the care system, she suspected Maxim's had been non-existent—ever since he was a young child and he had witnessed the way his mother had been neglected by his father. What better way to show him she loved him—without scaring him off—than to mark this special occasion? To show him he mattered to her.

Of course it had taken every ounce of her newfound confidence as the mistress of Château Durand to suggest it to Antoinette and the other staff but they had happily agreed to the idea.

This marriage didn't have to be an end, it could

be a beginning. They still had two and a half months before the baby was due and she already felt as if she belonged here.

'What do you think?' Cara asked, admiring her handiwork.

Antoinette leaned to one side to look and loosened her grip on the ladder. The slight wobble had Cara's body shifting.

'*Cara, descends tout de suite!*' The shout in French from behind her, demanding she get down immediately, startled Cara so much she swung round too fast.

The ladder tilted sharply to one side. Antoinette gasped.

Cara felt herself falling in slow motion, as she watched Maxim run towards her, his face a mask of panic. And pain.

Strong arms banded around her, breaking the fall. She inhaled a shuddering breath of pure relief. And caught the joyous scent of sandalwood soap and salty sweat.

Maxim. Maxim had saved her.

Her husband swore as she grasped his neck and clung on, pressing her face into the warmth of his pectoral muscles, feeling them tense and quiver under her nose.

Love rushed towards her, the threat forgotten.

'Cara, what were you doing? Are you mad?' He was shouting, his voice trembling.

But as she looked into his face, saw the dark eyes wild with concern, love flowed through her on a wave of hope. Why had she waited so long to show him how she felt about him?

'I'm sorry, Maxim. I was…' The surprise was ruined, but she let it go. 'It's your birthday, and we wanted to surprise you.'

'You… What?' He glanced around the room, taking in the bunches of balloons pinned to the cornicing, the banner she and Antoinette had made yesterday afternoon, the delicious *croquembouche* the chef had prepared on her instructions and the present she'd knitted herself over the last week, wrapped in paper and ribbon and arranged on a small side table with a bunch of early summer blooms she'd picked from the estate gardens that morning.

He placed her on her feet and stood back, his eyes widening as he studied the celebration she'd worked so hard on in complete silence. The muscle in his jaw tensed. He looked stunned, she realised.

And not happy.

She struggled to ignore the tightness in her chest at his reaction. He'd had a shock. They both had.

'Are you okay, *madame*?' Antoinette asked, still holding the ladder. 'I am so sorry I lost my grip.'

'Don't worry, Antoinette, it's—' Cara began, but Maxim interrupted.

'*Sortez*,' he said, the barked command for Antoinette to leave making both Cara and the maid jump. 'You are fired. I never want to see you on these premises again.'

The maid nodded and rushed out of the room in tears.

'Maxim, stop…' Cara touched his forearm. 'You can't fire Antoin—'

He swung round to grip her upper arms.

'Why? Why did you do this?' His voice broke on the words. This wasn't unhappiness, she realised, he looked undone, broken.

'Maxim, what's wrong?' she asked, the tightness like a vice now around her ribs.

Had she made a terrible mistake, confused her feelings with his? Projected emotions onto him that weren't there—had never been there?

He brushed a frustrated hand through his hair. 'You had no right.'

'I just wanted to do something for you, after all you've done for me,' she said, her voice shaking now at the sight of his distress.

'Any man would do it, to protect their child,' he said, the words clipped.

But when his eyes locked on hers, his gaze tortured, wild with pain, she knew she had to come clean about her real reasons for organising the celebration.

'No, they wouldn't, Maxim,' she answered,

trying to remain calm, trying to quell the riot of emotions pressing against her ribs, thundering in her heart.

Fear, panic, but most of all love.

'But you're right. That's not the real reason I did this,' she said, the truth pushing against her larynx and making her throat close. The moment had arrived when she couldn't hide behind that frightened, lonely child any longer.

'Then why?' he demanded.

'I wanted to celebrate your birthday, because I've fallen in love with you,' she said. 'And I want this to be a real marriage, for this house to be our home.'

He remained rigid, his eyes blank and unresponsive, so she found herself babbling the things he had never asked her about herself. And her past.

'I spent the whole of my childhood in a succession of foster homes,' she managed. 'Some were good, some were okay, some weren't. But I was never able to stay in any of them for very long. And when I came of age I spent years travelling around Europe, looking for something I finally found at La Maison de la Lune. I thought at first it was my friendship with Pierre, but it was much simpler than that—it was the home I made there. I discovered that I didn't need anyone else to make a place for me. I could make it for myself. But with you...' She swallowed down the lump of raw, unadulterated emotion. 'With you, I've discovered I want so much more than just a place to call my own. I want a real home. And I know, even though you've never said it, it's important to you too, or you wouldn't have reacted so strongly to becoming a father. Been so determined to care for me.' She could hear the painful hope in her voice, despite the rigid expression on his face. 'We could make this place into a home, Maxim. Make our marriage into a real marriage. For the baby, and for ourselves. All we have to do is admit that's what we need.'

She had hoped against hope to make a life for them both, but the last embers of that hope flickered and guttered out as she watched his blank expression harden.

'This marriage can never be real.'

'Why not?' she asked, desperation setting in.

'Because I will never love you back.'

'You don't have to love me, Maxim. Not yet,' she said, still trying to rescue a dream she knew had already died. 'All you have to do is open yourself to love.'

'I can't,' he said.

She nodded slowly, carefully, scared she was about to shatter into a million pieces at the finality in his statement. Not shatter, crumble into dust, feeling so insignificant, inconvenient, the way she'd been her whole life.

She hadn't asked him to love her, all she had asked for was the hope that one day he might. But he didn't even want to try. Anything she had to offer him would never be enough.

The little girl inside her who had watched her father walk away without a backward glance was screaming in pain. But the woman she had become simply nodded. 'Okay.'

She needed to leave before he saw her crumble, before he saw how much his rejection hurt. Or she would be nothing again.

It had taken her a lifetime to become somebody. And she couldn't let any man take that away from her. Not even him.

'You must not be upset,' he said stiffly. 'This is for the best.'

No, it's not.

'I need to be alone for a while,' she murmured.

He caught her wrist as she tried to leave. 'Cara, I'm sorry,' he said. 'But I thought you understood I can't offer you that.'

A spark of anger fired in her chest, and she clung to it. Anything to disguise the pain. 'You said to me once, Maxim, that you didn't need my pity,' she managed. 'I don't need yours either.'

She'd exposed herself to these feelings by accepting so little from him. And if this pain could teach her one thing, it was never to accept so little again.

'Where are you going?' he said from behind her as she walked away from him.

'To my rooms. I'd appreciate it if you didn't disturb me tonight,' she said, her voice coming from far away, as it occurred to her for the first time ever that she was glad they had separate bedrooms.

She couldn't make him love her. And she didn't want to. He'd seduced her with sex, but she had let him, revelling in the physical and wanting it to mean more when it never had. At least to him. All she could do now was repair her broken, foolishly misguided heart.

'Don't do anything foolish, Cara,' he said. 'We can talk more about this in the morning.'

She pressed her hand to her stomach, imagining the life inside her. And acknowledged how pathetically eager she would have been to take him up on the offer to talk about their relationship only minutes before. Why had she been prepared to accept whatever scraps of affection he was prepared to offer her?

She didn't feel tired as she headed up the stairs to her rooms, she felt exhausted, her feet like lumps of lead as she trudged up each step.

But one thing she did know: there was nothing left to talk about.

CHAPTER SEVENTEEN

'MONSIEUR DURAND, *MADAME* asked me to give you this.'

Maxim glanced up from his breakfast—the breakfast he hadn't been able to eat—to find the young maid he had fired the day before, and then reinstated because none of this was her fault, holding an envelope in her hand.

It was ten o'clock and he'd barely slept last night. He'd wanted to go to Cara's rooms a dozen times during the night, to soothe her and beg her to forgive him for his harsh words. To hold her in his arms and take the shattered pain in her eyes away the only way he knew how, by bringing her to the peak of ecstasy and watching her revel in her own pleasure. A pleasure only he could give her.

But he knew he couldn't, because that would only give her more false hope.

When she had told him last night of her childhood, the home she had been denied, all he'd been able to think about was her as a little girl, shunted from family to family without anywhere to belong. He'd wanted to hurt every single person who had rejected that little girl, had made her believe she wasn't enough.

But how could he punish them when he'd hurt her more? And made her believe she was the one who wasn't enough when it had always, always been him.

'*Merci*, Antoinette,' he said, remembering the girl's name and taking the envelope. 'Is my wife awake then?' he asked as he sliced open the envelope with his knife.

'The mistress woke hours ago, sir,' she said. 'She left at about nine o'clock.'

'She...left?' His fingers paused on the letter. 'Where did she go?' The hollow weight in his stomach turned into a sharp slice of panic.

'I do not know,' Antoinette said. 'She told me not to give you this letter, though, until ten o'clock. I think she took a car; she said she was going for a drive.'

No. No. No. No.

He flicked open the letter the girl had handed to him and read the words written in black ink.

Maxim,
    I'm sorry I can't be the wife you need. I

think it is best in the circumstances if we di-
vorce now.

I cannot bear to live with you and know
you feel nothing for me, when I feel so much
for you.

I hope you understand.

Cara x

His fingers shook, making the paper tremble.

She had run. He leapt out of his chair, the fear turning to terror—and the unbearable pain of longing. He forced his mind to engage. If she'd taken one of the estate's cars it would have a GPS tracker. He stormed out of the *château* towards the garage, praying each step of the way that she had not managed to get to the station already.

He couldn't lose her. Not again. Not like this. What had he done?

Cara took the turning into the short lane through the woods that led to La Maison de la Lune. She'd been driving aimlessly for over an hour, trying to get her thoughts in order before she went home. Not home, she thought miserably.

Back to Château Durand to talk to Maxim about the divorce.

He would have received her letter by now. She'd left her phone at home precisely so he couldn't contact her. But she would have to go back soon. She didn't want him to worry unnecessarily.

She wasn't even sure how she had ended up here. She knew Maxim would have knocked down La Maison last September when she'd run away from him, but even so she hoped that just being in this place, where everything had begun, might help her get some perspective on her pain—and her grief—at the end of their marriage.

Despite everything, she was still struggling to accept that everything she'd believed about her and Maxim's relationship—the intimacy she had believed had been growing between them—had been wrong.

The car took the short bend in the road through the woods but, as she steeled herself for the empty plot that awaited her, she spotted a shape through the trees that had her heart—her bruised and battered heart—bouncing into her throat.

The house—the house she had once loved so dearly—still stood. The shutters were closed, the door boarded up, the flowers she'd planted in the boxes on the windowsills wilted. But the structure itself—the stone walls, the wooden gables, the red slates of the roof—were all still there, just as she'd left them that morning, when she'd run away from Maxim—and, she now realised, feelings that even then had terrified her.

She drove into the yard in the SUV she'd borrowed and braked, then rubbed her tired eyes. Was she dreaming, imagining this?

Why would Maxim not have destroyed the house? He'd been so determined to do it all those months ago—she now knew because of the cruel way his father had treated him and his mother—and, after discovering the full extent of Pierre's cruelty, she didn't blame him.

So why was it still here, whole and solid and, from the way the yard had been brushed free of autumn leaves, also cared for in the months since her departure?

She got out of the car, walked to the door and laid her cheek against the worn wood. After all the months she'd lived here with Pierre, all she could remember about her life inside these walls was that one forbidden night with Maxim. The hunger, the panic, the joy and then the pain. But most of all the tenderness that she'd failed to acknowledge then, but couldn't help but acknowledge now.

The tears that she'd shed during the night returned. God, it hurt to know that even though he'd rejected her, she loved him still. And she knew she always would—that was why she'd asked him for a divorce. She couldn't go on living with him, sleeping with him, knowing that he would never be able to love her back.

She heard the purr of an engine, getting louder, cutting through the chirping cheerfulness of a goldfinch's song. As she turned Maxim's car drove into the yard. The squeal of brakes was followed by the slam of the car door as he jumped out.

'Cara…you're here…you didn't run?' he said. His eyes were wild, as wild as they had been yesterday in the moments before he had told her he didn't love her, when he'd saved her from falling.

She wiped the tears off her cheeks. 'Of course not,' she said, shocked when he ran across the yard towards her. 'I just needed some space.'

Suddenly she was in his arms and he was hugging her so tightly her heart was hammering against her ribs like a jackhammer.

'*Ne me quitte pas, ne me quitte jamais,*' he murmured against her hair, his tone urgent, desperate. *Don't leave me, don't ever leave me.*

'Maxim?' She pulled back, her heart swelling in her chest and clattering against her ribs. 'I wouldn't have run away. Not again. Not now.'

He sunk to his knees, clasped her thighs, pressing his head into the mound of her belly. 'I thought… I thought you had left me.'

She sunk her fingers into his hair, drew his face up, and saw something in his eyes that had her swollen heart bursting in her chest. She glanced back at the house—the first home she had known.

But that home had meant nothing until she had welcomed him into it.

'Maxim, why didn't you destroy La Maison?'

'Because I couldn't,' he said, his expression stark, naked with the longing he had never allowed her to see, until this moment. 'After you left it was the only thing I had that reminded me of you.' He swore softly and dropped his head. 'My revenge against him seemed unimportant once I had lost you,' he said. 'I don't want to lose you again. I can't.'

Her heart did a giddy leap, despite the hopelessness in his voice.

Had she been wrong to give up so easily, to believe what he'd told her instead of following her own instincts, her own emotions?

Gripping his cheeks, she forced his gaze back to hers. 'Maxim, you don't have to lose me. I love you,' she said again, but she refused to bask in the fierce emotion in his eyes. She couldn't settle for less, the way she had settled so often before. 'But you made it very clear yesterday you can never love me back. Is that really the truth?'

He shook his head, but his expression became bleak. 'I lied,' he said, his voice full of emotion as he covered her hands with his and stood up. 'Because I'm a coward,' he said, dragging her hands from his cheeks. 'Because I'm afraid of what I feel for you.' He placed their joined hands over her belly. 'And for our child. Because I am scared I can never be enough. And that I will fail you, the way I failed my mother.'

Cara looked stunned, Maxim realised, but so beautiful his heart broke just looking at her. She still loved him, but how could he take comfort from that until she knew the truth—until she knew what he'd done all those years ago? How could he ever hope to deserve her love if he did not tell her what he had done to his own mother?

'How did you fail your mother, Maxim?' she said, the sweet compassion in her eyes wrenching the truth he had never wanted to reveal out of his mouth.

'She was frail, fragile, as I told you, ever since I was a young boy. My birth and the miscarriages she had suffered had hurt her, both physically and mentally. She had dark moods, days when she could barely function, and when that happened she needed me to cook for her, to talk to her, to get her out of bed. The day I came here…' he looked at the house he had always hated, until he had found his salvation inside it '…to tell my father I knew I was his son. I was so excited. It was my birthday. I was fifteen and I believed myself a man. I thought he would want me. But he didn't. And I was so devastated, so hurt and angry, I took it out on her. I left Burgundy, even though she begged me not to. Even though I knew she would struggle on her own. She needed me and I left anyway. Five months later, she was dead.'

Once the words were out, he waited to see the love in Cara's eyes curdle and die, to turn into the disgust with himself he had felt for so many years. But the warmth in his wife's deep blue eyes didn't falter or fade, it didn't even flicker, she simply absorbed his confession and then wrapped her arms around his waist, pulling him away from the darkness—and back into the light.

'Maxim, that's madness. You weren't responsible for her death. You were her son, not her parent. Whatever you did or didn't do for her, you weren't responsible for her pain or her fragility, or her depression.' She glanced over her shoulder at the house he'd saved because he couldn't bear to lose the one thing he had that would remind him of their one night together. 'If anyone was responsible,' she added as she turned back to him, 'it was your father. He didn't deserve a son like you.'

Her faith in him seemed to seep into his bones as they stood in the sunlight together. He held her too tightly. But he knew he wouldn't be able to loosen his grip. Not for a while.

'Can you give me another chance?' he asked. 'To make this marriage a real marriage. To become a real father to our son. To figure out how to love you.'

It was the hardest but also the easiest question he'd ever asked of anyone.

The bright smile she sent him reached into his soul and lightened his heart, until it bobbed into his throat.

'Yes,' she said. 'But first I want something from you.'

'Whatever it is, it is yours,' he said, knowing he would be willing to give her anything she desired. If she wanted a palace—if she wanted two—he would buy it for her. She was worth every penny he had, every second of his time it took to earn those pennies. Whatever he had to do to be worthy of her love, he would do it.

'I want you to promise that you will stay in my bed until morning,' she said.

'That is all?' He blinked, baffled not just by the simplicity of her request but by the strength of the wonder that barrelled through him at the thought of waking up with her soft body in his arms and never having to let go of her again. Ever.

She nodded.

He threw back his head and laughed, the joy—that he had found her and would never ever have to lose her—almost too much to bear.

'Do I have your promise?' she asked, her voice

stern but her eyes sparkling with the same joy exploding in his chest.

'My beautiful wife,' he murmured as he lowered his head to hers, ready to kiss them both into oblivion then kick in the door of the old farmhouse and carry her upstairs to the bedroom they had shared all those months ago, 'I promise I will hold you until morning, every day for the rest of our lives.'

EPILOGUE

'Let me take *le bébé*. You must sleep.'

'Go for it, Papa.' Cara smiled as her husband leant across the wide double bed they had shared all night, every night, for the first time three months ago—the day their marriage had become a real marriage—and scooped their week-old son into his arms.

Tucking the tiny body against his naked chest, he placed a firm hand against the baby's back and crooned in a deep, gentle voice, 'Shh, *mon petit garçon*, it is time to sleep. Your mother has fed you enough for one night.'

The baby stopped fidgeting on hearing his father's voice, and gave a loud burp.

Cara chuckled wearily.

'Our son is very greedy,' Maxim murmured, but she could hear the fierce pride in his voice. 'Hopefully, he will give us both some rest now.'

'Fingers crossed,' Cara said around a huge yawn. Tucking her now empty breast back into her maternity bra, she snuggled back under the bed's summer quilt, contentment rolling through on a wave of fatigue as Maxim whispered instructions to his son and the baby's eyes drifted shut. At last.

The fatigue was joined by a wave of love—for both the guys in her life—which crested as her heart beat a strong, steady tattoo against her ribs.

Seriously, was there anything more wonderful than watching this man become the father he was always meant to be? How could Maxim ever have believed he wasn't capable of loving her, or their child?

Her husband climbed out of the bed and carried their baby in strong arms to the bassinet, then laid him down gently on his back. She forced herself to stay awake so she could watch the familiar ritual.

She couldn't help noticing the muscles in his backside flexing beneath the pyjama bottoms he had started wearing a few weeks ago—when she'd been so huge that sex had become impossible. She felt the familiar flutter of appreciation. It would be quite a while yet before she'd want to act on it—hello, ten hours of labour!—but she could still enjoy the show as Maxim concentrated on stroking his son's cheek to lull him into a deeper sleep.

She gave another jaw-breaking yawn and noticed the glow of the summer dawn through the large bedroom's shutters. She should probably go to sleep too. In two hours, three at the most, their insatiable son would want another feed.

Instead she blinked furiously to keep her tired eyes open, as she waited for Maxim to return to the bed. She had something important she wanted to ask him.

At last, satisfied that their son had finally fallen into a deep enough sleep, Maxim padded back to the bed. Climbing in beside her, he dropped a quick kiss onto her nose. 'Go to sleep, Madame Durand.'

'I will…but, Maxim, I've got another name for you first.'

They'd spoken—or rather argued—about what to call their son on and off for over three months now. Which had basically consisted of her coming up with names and Maxim vetoing them all. She loved that he was so determined to get it right, but seriously, their son would be in university before they came up with one they could agree on if they didn't get a move on.

'And this cannot wait until morning?' he sighed, yawning himself, and then wrapped his arm around her shoulders to pull her against his side.

'No.' She snuggled into his embrace, the scent of sandalwood soap and baby's milk that clung to his skin making the flutter of appreciation become a definite hum—and the warmth in her heart spread.

'Okay,' he sighed. 'What is your latest terrible suggestion?' he said.

'Stop it.' She gave him a playful slap. 'My suggestions are not terrible.'

'Hugo? Eugene? *Mortimer*?' he teased.

'Mortimer was a joke.'

'And the other two?' he said, pressing his lips into her hair in one of the many absent gestures of affection he always showed her, that she had come to adore. 'For them there is no excuse.'

'How about Pascal?' she blurted out.

He stilled, the easy smile dropping from his lips in the half-light. She could hear his heart thumping against her ear. And feel hers beating in time.

He frowned down at her. 'What made you think of this name?' he said, his tone gruff. But she could tell, from the emotion in his voice, which he never hid from her any more, that he had already guessed the connection.

'You said once that your mother's surname was Pascale.'

He stared at her and her heart thundered.

'You remembered this?' he asked, his voice raw with surprise but also rough with love.

She nodded, peering up at him. 'Do you like it?'

He brushed a hand over her hair, then leant down to cover her lips with his, the intensity of the kiss all the answer she needed.

When he drew back his face was a picture of raw emotion. 'Pascal Evans Durand,' he murmured softly, his voice rich with love as he tried out the name. '*J'adore*,' he said. 'But not as much as I adore him… And you, Cara.'

* * * * *

Wrapped up in the drama of
A Forbidden Night with the Housekeeper?
*Enter Heidi Rice's passionate world
with these other stories!*

Claiming My Untouched Mistress
Contracted as His Cinderella Bride
Claimed for the Desert Prince's Heir
My Shocking Monte Carlo Confession

Available now!